P9-EMG-866
ITMf Lot 4
SC
8 Apr05
45.82
45.82

Aunt Dimity: Snowbound

Aunt Dimity: Snowbound

Nancy Atherton

THORNDIKE
CHIVERS

This Large Print edition is published by Thorndike Press®, Waterville, Maine USA and by BBC Audiobooks, Ltd, Bath, England.

Published in 2004 in the U.S. by arrangement with Viking Penguin, a member of Penguin Group (USA) Inc.

Published in 2004 in the U.K. by arrangement with the author.

U.S. Hardcover 0-7862-6268-0 (Mystery)
U.K. Hardcover 0-7540-9677-7 (Chivers Large Print)
U.K. Softcover 0-7540-9678-5 (Camden Large Print)

The text of this Large Print edition is unabridged. Other aspects of the book may vary from the original edition.

Set in 16 pt. Plantin by Carleen Stearns.

Printed in the United States on permanent paper.

British Library Cataloguing-in-Publication Data available

ISBN 0-7862-6268-0 (lg. print : hc : alk. paper)

For
Wendy Lindboe,
rambler

One

The holidays nearly killed me. While my clever lawyer husband used work as an excuse to avoid all but the most pressing social engagements, I flung myself at Christmas with the carefree abandon of a lemming rushing headlong toward a cliff.

While Bill barricaded himself behind legal files in our honey-colored cottage, I volunteered for every committee and attended every party given in or near Finch, the tiny English village we'd called home for the past six years. I adorned St. George's Church with evergreen boughs, warbled carols on a multitude of unsuspecting doorsteps, constructed scenery for the nativity play, prepared our four-year-old twin sons for their stage debuts as singing shepherds, baked enough angel cookies to choke a reindeer, and gave nearly as many parties — for children as well as adults — as I attended.

Even when the holidays were over, even when we flew to Boston in January for our annual visit with Bill's family, I couldn't shake the tinsel from my hair. While Bill spent his days enjoying cozy chats before the fire with his delightful father, I took the twins sledding and skating and sleigh-riding and compounded my folly by whisking Bill off on sentimental journeys to revisit old friends and dine out in favorite restaurants every evening.

By the time we returned to the cottage in mid-February, I was a burnt-out husk of my formerly jolly self. I winced when our sons burst into song, my gorge rose at the thought of nibbling another angel cookie, and I could scarcely bring myself to repack our Christmas decorations because the mere sight of them made my head throb. I was, in short, the pitiful victim of a self-induced holiday hangover.

Emma Harris had no trouble diagnosing my condition. As my closest neighbor and dearest friend in England she'd seen it all before, and when she found me lying listlessly on the bamboo chaise longue beneath the apple tree in my back garden, she knew exactly what had happened.

Appearances notwithstanding, I wasn't merely lounging. Since Bill was catching up on paperwork at his office in Finch, and Annelise, the twins' saintly nanny, was spending the afternoon with her mother on the family farm, I'd retired to the back garden to keep a sleepy eye on Will and Rob, who were busily building highways in the well-mulched vegetable patch.

Although I wasn't prepared to receive visitors, I was always glad to see Emma, who'd strolled over from her manor house to welcome me home and bring me up to date on local gossip. As she called a cheery hello to Will and Rob and seated herself on the deck chair opposite mine, I found myself envying her vitality. It was a gorgeous day, unseasonably warm and sunny, but I could barely summon the energy to acknowledge her arrival.

Emma surveyed me critically before commenting, "You've been burning the yule log at both ends. *Again.*"

I hung my head, knowing what she would say next.

"What happened to the simple family Christmas you raved about?" she asked, right on cue. "What happened to staying at home and making angel cookies —"

"Please don't mention angel cookies," I muttered as my stomach whimpered.

"— and singing carols around your own hearth?" Emma went on. "What happened to a simple Christmas in the cottage with

Bill and the boys?"

"Bill stayed in the cottage," I reminded her, "but the boys and I kind of . . . didn't." I held a hand out to her pleadingly. "I can't help it, Emma. I'm addicted to holly. When sleigh bells ring I lose my head. I can't keep myself from hopping up next to Santa and grabbing the reins. It's a fun ride, truly it is, and Will and Rob loved every minute of it."

"I'm sure they did," said Emma. "But you're a wreck."

"I'm not the perkiest elf on the block," I admitted.

"You're about as perky as a tree stump." Emma pursed her lips and gazed thoughtfully toward the meadow beyond the garden wall. A pleasant silence ensued, a silence that was suddenly shattered by the sharp snap of her fingers as she exclaimed, "I know what'll pull you out of your funk!"

"A large box of chocolates?" I murmured.

"No. Not chocolates." Emma got to her feet, took two paces, and turned to face me. "You're going for a walk."

I sank deeper into the cushioned chaise longue. "I'd prefer the chocolates."

Emma shook her head decisively. "You have to give energy to get energy," she said.

"I'm not talking about running a marathon, Lori. I'm talking about a stroll through some lovely countryside. Solitude, fresh air, and communion with nature — that's what you need."

I gazed pointedly at the apple tree's bare branches. "Not much nature to commune with, this time of year."

"You'd be surprised," said Emma. "If you're lucky you'll see rabbits, deer, woodpeckers, owls — maybe even a few foxes. And the early lambing is underway." She took an invigorating breath and let it out in a whoosh. "There's nothing like the sight of a gamboling lamb to refresh the spirits."

"Do lambs gambol in snow?" I inquired dryly. "I mean, Emma, it's *February.* Last I heard, February wasn't considered the balmiest month of the year in jolly old England."

"It hasn't been so bad this year." Emma swept a hand toward the clear blue sky. "We haven't had a drop of rain or a flake of snow since December, and the meteorologists predict that the fine weather will last till the end of the month."

"I can't disappear for the rest of the month," I protested.

"How about one day, then?" Emma proposed. "Surely you can manage to escape for one day. Bill won't mind, and Annelise is more than capable of looking after the boys while you're gone."

"Let me think about it," I said, nestling my head into the cushions.

Emma regarded me sternly. "You're not doing the twins any good, sitting there like a lump."

I knew that my best friend was taking advantage of my tender maternal instincts by inserting the boys into the conversation, but I also knew that she was telling the truth. Will and Rob deserved a wide-awake and active mummy, a mummy who would get down in the dirt and play trucks with them, not a Drowsy Drusilla, yawning at them from the sidelines. Perhaps a walk *would* wake me up. Perhaps the sight of gamboling lambs *would* refresh my spirits. If nothing else, it would get me off of the chaise longue.

Emma must have sensed an opening in my defenses because she began to press her case. "I've got the perfect trail for you. I hiked it last summer. It's easy terrain, the path's well-marked, and it's not far from here. You can stop along the way for a picnic lunch. I'll drop you off at the trail head and be waiting for you when you reach the other end."

"Why don't you come along?" I suggested.

"Because you need peace and quiet, that's why." Emma resumed her seat. "We've hiked together before, Lori. I know what you're like on the trail. Talk, talk, talk, from beginning to end. You need a break from people, and that includes me."

I was forced to admit that she had a point. Emma and I had much in common — like me, she was a transplanted Yank with two children — but there were differences as well. Emma's husband was English, for one thing, while Bill was American. Her children were nearly grown, whereas mine weren't quite finished being babies. She weighed every decision carefully, while I tended to be a bit impulsive. And although we were the best of friends, we weren't the best of hiking companions.

To me, a hike was a chance to release the mind and engage the senses. I loved to ramble aimlessly, savoring whatever surprises nature had in store for me along the way. I believed that *lost* was a relative term because all trails led somewhere, particularly in England, which was, after all, a very crowded little island where you could scarcely walk ten steps without tripping over a pub, a farmhouse, or a charming village. I'd gotten lost so often that Emma had, only half-jokingly, offered to attach a homing device to my day pack, but I'd refused. Getting lost on a beautiful spring day was, for me, part of the fun.

Emma, on the other hand, belonged to the map-and-compass crowd. She owned a veritable library of Ordnance Survey maps and never left home without a half dozen in her day pack. To Emma, hiking was an intellectual activity, a mission to be accomplished, a puzzle to be solved. While on the trail, she seemed to spend more time studying maps than gazing upon the natural beauty surrounding her. If she got lost — which she did, even when I wasn't around to distract her with talk, talk, talk — she felt she'd failed. It seemed to me that the only advantage her method of navigation had over mine was that, at the end of the day, she could figure out exactly where she'd gone wrong.

The more I thought about it, the more I agreed with Emma: If the proposed walk was to have any beneficial effects, it would best be taken without her company.

"How long is this trail of yours?" I asked.

"Nine miles, give or take a few hundred yards," Emma replied. "You'll be able to manage it in five hours, six at the most. I'll pack your lunch for you," she offered. "I'll even pack your day pack."

I smiled. "Be sure to tuck in a few hundred maps, will you? In case I end up in Borneo or Venezuela . . ."

"I'll put in a map of the trail." Emma leaned forward and patted my arm. "But I promise you, you won't get lost this time. Honestly, it's a simple, straightforward route. I'll show it to you on the map. There's only one turning, and," she sailed on, blithely uttering the curse that had doomed travelers for centuries, "you can't miss it."

Her enthusiasm was so infectious that the curse drifted past me, unnoticed, and in all innocence I agreed to spend a day hiking her straightforward trail, providing Bill agreed that he could live without me for five hours (six at the most). I paid no attention whatsoever to the tiny voice screaming in the back of my mind, warning me that a simple walk could be every bit as treacherous as a simple Christmas.

Two

Annelise took the news of my impending departure in stride, and Bill's most memorable comment about Emma's cure for my holiday hangover was that he wished he'd thought of it himself.

"Go," he told me when we sat down to dinner that evening. "Take advantage of the good weather while it lasts. The fresh air will put the bounce back in your step. But bring your cell phone, just in case."

"In case I get hopelessly lost?" I said, lifting an eyebrow.

My husband responded with more gallantry than truth. "In case you discover someplace so glorious that you can't resist the urge to describe it to me on the spot."

"I'll bring the cell phone," I promised, and rewarded his gallantry with a kiss. "Care to come along?"

"I'd love to, Lori, but I can't," he said. "You know how work piles up over the holidays. I haven't seen the top of my desk since we got back from Boston."

I felt a pang of disappointment, but I tried to conceal it. I couldn't back out now — Emma had already organized my day pack and prepared my picnic lunch. Apart from that, Bill was so pleased with the ingenious plan that I couldn't bring myself to admit that I was having second thoughts.

Did I really want to spend a day in the woods, alone? The past couple of months had been intensely social. Could I handle five or six hours with no one to talk to but a handful of gamboling lambs? I suddenly felt as if my nearest and dearest were thrusting me, cold turkey, into an isolation chamber.

"Lori," Bill said, taking note of my furrowed brow, "you don't have to go if you don't want to."

"I *do* want to go," I said. "But I'm not sure I want to go by myself."

"Take Aunt Dimity," he suggested. "You can chat with her if you get too lonely."

"What a good idea!" My brow smoothed. "Communing with nature is right up her alley."

"Take Reginald, too," Bill said. "Reg can ride with his head sticking out of your pack, and Aunt Dimity'll fit inside. They don't weigh much, and Emma won't have to add extra food for them."

"They'll be perfect trail mates," I agreed, and passed the roast potatoes to my husband, beaming.

A stranger eavesdropping on our dinnertime conversation could be forgiven for assuming that Bill and I were clinically insane. Why couldn't Reginald walk on his own two feet? the stranger would wonder. And how on earth will they stash nature-loving Aunt Dimity *inside* a day pack?

The stranger would no doubt be relieved to learn that Reginald was a stuffed animal I'd had since childhood, a small, powder-pink flannel rabbit who would be perfectly content to view the passing scenery from the confines of my pack. An explanation of Aunt Dimity's extreme portability, however, would only confirm the stranger's suspicion that my husband and I were a pair of raving loonies.

Easy explanations were hard to come by when discussing Aunt Dimity. As a child, I'd known her as the main character in a series of bedtime stories invented by my mother. I was astonished to learn many years later that my mother had based her fictional heroine on a decidedly nonfictional Englishwoman named Dimity Westwood.

My mother had met Dimity Westwood in London, where both women had served their respective countries during the Second World War. They'd become fast friends during those dark years and had shared the stories of their postwar lives in letters that had flown back and forth across the Atlantic by the hundreds.

I first learned of their friendship after Dimity Westwood's death, when I found that she had bequeathed to me the precious correspondence, a honey-colored cottage in the Cotswolds, a comfortable fortune, and a curious journal bound in dark-blue leather.

It was through the journal that I finally came to know my mother's dearest friend. When I opened the blue journal, its blank pages came alive with Dimity's graceful script, an old-fashioned copperplate taught in the village school at a time when motorcars were still a rare and wondrous sight. Although I'd nearly fainted the first time Dimity's words had scrolled across the page, I'd long since grown accustomed to her extraordinary, ongoing presence in my life.

But I'd never try to explain it to a stranger.

"I'll fetch Reginald and the journal from

the study after dinner," I said, refilling Bill's wineglass. "I'll recharge the cell phone overnight and be ready to leave first thing in the morning."

"Bravo." Bill raised his glass to me. "To the great explorer. May your hiking boots never grow heavier."

I laughed and touched my glass to his. I was confident, now, that my day on the trail would be as enjoyable as everyone else expected it to be.

True to her word, Emma turned up at the crack of dawn to drive me to the trailhead. Morning was my least perky time of day, so I ignored the twisting, turning route she selected to reach our destination and granted myself the gift of an extra forty winks. Emma nudged me awake when we arrived.

"I don't know how you can sleep on such a beautiful day," she scolded. "You're a sad case."

"Tragic," I agreed, stifling a yawn.

"Look, Lori, I don't mean to browbeat you," said Emma. "If you don't feel up to tackling —"

"I'll be fine," I broke in, turning to lift my pack from the backseat.

"If you say so." Emma eyed me doubtfully. "But for heaven's sake, stick to the path. I'll be waiting for you when you reach the other end."

I got out of the car, waved until Emma had driven out of sight, then turned in a slow circle to take stock of the day.

It was beautiful. The morning air was crisp but not frigid, with the merest hint of a rising breeze to ruffle the short dark curls that had escaped my stocking cap. A ragged veil of high clouds hung across the sparkling blue sky, and the only sound to be heard was the dry rustle of dead leaves clinging to the winter-bare branches of the surrounding trees.

A few yards away and slightly to my right, a tall wooden post marked with a painted arrow indicated the trailhead. I could see from where I stood that I'd have to clamber over a stile to reach the actual trail, but I didn't mind a bit of clambering. The crisp air had banished my drowsiness. I felt alert, alive, and ready for anything.

"Emma would be pleased," I declared. "Her walking cure seems to be working already — and I haven't even taken a step." Grinning, I slung my pack's padded straps comfortably over my shoulders, shoved my woolly gloves into my pocket, and unzipped my lightweight down jacket. The weather was so mild that my cream-colored cotton sweater and blue jeans would provide ample warmth once I started walking.

"Hang on tight, Reg," I said, reaching up to touch my bunny's ears. "A stile awaits."

I hiked for three hours without stopping. The trail skirted the edge of several disappointingly lambless fields before descending gradually into a densely wooded valley. As I left the neatly hedgerowed pastures behind, I reflected with pleasure on the general tidiness of the English countryside.

Every square inch of Cotswolds soil had, at one time or another over the past few thousand years, been plowed by farmers, grazed by sheep, or rearranged en masse by power-crazed landscape architects. The result was a civilized countryside, a countryside that soothed, and while some might find it tediously tame, I found it reassuring. There were those who enjoyed teetering on the brink of fathomless chasms while fending off hoards of grizzlies, and then there were the rest of us. I had no desire to hack a path through dark, undiscovered jungles. I preferred to walk where generations had walked before, and where the likelihood of running into large carnivorous creatures was relatively remote. Well-trodden paths allowed me the luxury of daydreaming.

Daydreaming, alas, is not a sound aid to navigation. A familiar sense of chagrin crept over me when I paused to glance at Emma's map and realized that, thanks to the travelers' curse — and, perhaps, to my own inattentiveness — I'd missed the unmissable turning. Instead of going left and climbing back out of the valley, I'd gone straight and hiked all the way down to the valley floor.

I should have swung around and retraced my steps right then and there, but I was seized by a desire for adventure — and secure in the knowledge that I had a cell phone handy — so I strode on, savoring the thump of my boots on the hard ground, the silence of the sleeping trees, and the occasional glimpse of a bird who'd forgotten to fly south for the winter. I was so absorbed in the sheer physical exhilaration of walking that I failed to notice the storm clouds gathering overhead. It wasn't until a downy flake brushed my cheek that I became aware of others drifting like thistledown from a sky that had turned leaden.

"So much for Emma's forecasting skills," I grumbled, stopping to tuck Reginald safely inside my pack. "You want to know why it hasn't snowed since December, Reg? Because I haven't been hiking!" Reginald's black button eyes gleamed sympathetically as I drew the pack's flap over his ears. "Ah, well," I added, reshouldering my pack, "maybe it'll blow over."

As I uttered the word *blow* a gust of wind buffeted the trees. Chuckling grimly at Mother Nature's little joke, I zipped my jacket and turned to climb out of the valley, hoping against hope that I'd find my way back to the proper trail before her mood turned ugly.

The blizzard hit about ten minutes later. It seemed to come from everywhere at once, barreling through the valley like a whirling avalanche, turning the nearest trees into faint gray smudges, and burying the path in a rapidly thickening layer of snow. A vicious wind lanced through my jeans, and bitter, swirling flurries stung my face. I was deafened by the wind's howl, blinded by the biting snow, and utterly alone. There was no point in putting out an SOS to Bill — what would I tell him? "I don't know where I am but come and get me"? So I put on my woolly gloves and forged ahead.

I'd forged no more than fifty yards when

a snow-covered tree root tripped me up and sent me slithering down a short but knobbly bank and into a slimy, snow-soaked pile of last year's leaves. Bruised, winded, and very much annoyed, I rolled onto my knees and found that I'd landed within arm's reach of an imposing, ivy-clad stone gatepost. It was one of a pair that stood on either side of what appeared to be a narrow lane. As I scrambled to my feet the wind snatched at the ivy, revealing a darker square against the pale Cotswolds stone. I stepped forward, pushed the brittle leaves aside, and saw two words inscribed on a bronze plaque.

"Ladythorne Abbey," I whispered, and thanked my lucky stars.

I'd seen the words before, on Emma's map. They'd been printed in miniscule letters, suggesting that Ladythorne Abbey was nothing more than an abandoned ruin, but even a ruin would provide some shelter from the storm. More important, it would give me a point of reference I could pass along to Bill via the cell phone.

Heartened by visions of my gallant husband riding our canary-yellow Range Rover to my rescue, I put my head down and turned up the lane toward Ladythorne Abbey.

Three

I made good speed up the lane. It was easy to follow, straight and level, with steep banks on either side, and the ferocious wind helped, too, pushing at my back like a giant hand, as if eager to hurry me on my way. Nevertheless, the snow was shin-deep and rising by the time I spied the ghostly outline of a building dead ahead.

Ladythorne Abbey didn't seem to be a ruin. As I slogged forward, I caught snow-veiled glimpses of a long, low-lying building made of pale gray stone and set about with quirky bays, mullioned windows, and oddly angled roofs. A slender bell tower rose from one end of the building, a colonnaded cloister extended from the other, and in the center I saw a sweep of stairs leading to an entryway framed by Gothic arches. The staircase was covered with a pristine blanket of snow.

The abbey looked as if it had grown in stages over centuries, collecting bits and pieces by whim instead of following the dictates of a master plan. I suspected that it was one of the monastic properties that had been confiscated by Henry VIII and bestowed upon a worthy supporter in the sixteenth century. The cloister in particular seemed the perfect setting for a procession of medieval meditating monks. If I hadn't been so cold and wet and miserable, I would have taken a leisurely stroll around the place to explore its nooks and crannies.

But I *was* cold and wet, and becoming more miserable by the second, so I decided to postpone the leisurely stroll and concentrate instead on finding a way to get inside, out of the storm. I'd stumbled a half step toward the snow-covered stairs when I saw a splash of red in the cloister. It was the first drop of color I'd seen since the blizzard had begun — and it was moving.

"Hey!" I shouted, turning toward the cloister. "*Hey!* Wait up!"

The red blur came to a halt. As I drew closer I saw a shapeless figure carrying a full-sized backpack. The backpack was made of a brilliant red fabric bordered by an unusual pattern of writhing black flames. The strangely sinister fabric seemed more suited to a biker than a hiker, but the rest of the backpacker's gear was conventional enough: heavy boots, bulky gray parka, baggy weatherproof trousers, black balaclava, and wraparound sunglasses. The backpacker was so well bundled against the cold that even at close range I couldn't tell if it was a man or a woman. Only the tip of his or her nose was visible between the sunglasses and the balaclava. I identified deeply with the exposed nose; it was nearly as red as the backpack.

"Hi," I said cheerfully, as I stepped into the cloister. "Lovely weather we're having, isn't it?"

"Lovely," the backpacker agreed in a muffled voice. "Do you live here?"

"No," I said. "I was kind of hoping you did."

"No." The backpacker began walking toward the back of the house. "Thought I'd look for a rear entrance."

"Have you tried the front door?" I asked.

"No one answered," said the backpacker. "Come on."

"I'm coming," I said, and as my new companion plowed a path through the snow for me to follow, I wondered fleetingly how he or she had approached the front door without leaving tracks in the staircase's smooth blanket of snow.

The cloistered walkway opened onto a

cobbled courtyard enclosed by various outbuildings that seemed to be sinking rapidly beneath the rising drifts. The backpacker ignored the outbuildings and headed directly for a plain wooden door set in a section of the main house that projected into the courtyard. When we reached the door, I grasped the handle eagerly, but it refused to budge.

"Locked," I muttered.

"We'll see about that."

I stood back and watched with growing astonishment as the backpacker reached into a side pocket of the flaming red backpack, produced a short-handled pry bar, and inserted it between the door and the jamb.

"What are you doing?" I said, taken aback. "You'll damage the door, won't you?"

"Would you prefer to stay out here?" my fearless leader retorted.

"B-but . . . what if someone's home?" I sputtered.

"We'll advise them to answer their front door next time." With an excruciating crunch, the wooden door's lock gave way, and the backpacker strode inside.

I glanced over my shoulder, half expecting a police constable to leap from a snowdrift and arrest us for breaking and entering, then chided myself for being such a ninny and stepped across the threshold. If I *did* end up in court, I reasoned, my lawyer husband could surely make a case for extenuating circumstances.

I closed the courtyard door behind me and paused to savor the sensation of having five inches of solid oak between me and the biting wind. As I wiped icy droplets from my face, however, I realized that I could still see my breath. Ladythorne Abbey's current owner clearly wasn't wasting money on heating bills.

Not that I blamed him; it would have cost a fortune to heat the room we'd broken into. It was a kitchen, a huge kitchen with a vaulted ceiling, six pointy-arched Gothic windows, a polished, black-and-white-tile floor, and connecting doors piercing each wall.

A great stone trough of a sink built on brick legs rested beneath the Gothic windows, with a stone draining board at one end, a wooden plate-drying rack at the other, and in between a pair of antiquated porcelain taps and a grid of copper pipes running its length. I tried the taps and breathed a sigh of relief when water splashed into the sink — cold water only, but cold running water was better than none at all.

Two vast dressers faced one another across the room, one painted white and laden with crockery, the other painted brown and filled with beaten copper pots, pans, and various large cooking utensils. A sturdy oak table, scarred with use and big enough to seat ten, occupied the center of the room, and the far wall held an elaborate black-leaded Victorian range set into a whitewashed chimney breast.

A simple brass chandelier hung from the ceiling and brass light fixtures protruded from the walls, but when I flicked the light switches beside the courtyard door, nothing happened.

"Storm must've taken out the electricity," I said, brushing the snow from my jeans. "I'm Lori Shepherd, by the way."

"Wendy Walker," said the backpacker.

While I concentrated on snow-removal, Wendy slipped her backpack from her shoulders and leaned it against the white dresser. She wisely kept her parka on, but removed her sunglasses, revealing a pair of blue-gray eyes beneath a fringe of fluffy gray bangs. When she pulled the balaclava from her head, she loosed a waist-length cloud of gray hair that framed a round, wind-reddened face. She looked as if she might be a few years older than me, in her late thirties or early forties.

"I'm incredibly pleased to meet you, Wendy," I said effusively. "I wasn't looking forward to weathering the storm on my own."

"It wouldn't have been much fun." Wendy tucked the pry bar, sunglasses, and balaclava into her pack, twisted her long hair into a knot at the nape of her neck, and began moving from door to door, surveying the rooms that opened off of the kitchen. When she reached the first door she asked, over her shoulder, "Are you from the States?"

"Yep." I took off my day pack and placed it on the oak table. "I was born and raised in Chicago, but I've lived in England for the past six years. You?"

"Long Island, New York." She peered into what appeared to be a darkened corridor, closed the door, and moved on to the next. "Do you live near here?"

I had no clear memory of the route Emma had taken, so I answered as best I could. "I live near a small village about" — I picked a number at random — "twenty miles from here. I've never been to Ladythorne before, though. I didn't even know it existed, not as a complete house. I thought it was a ruin."

"That's what it looks like on the map," said Wendy. "But maps can be misleading."

"Did you get lost, too?" I asked.

"The storm threw me off course," Wendy replied.

"Me, too," I said, half-truthfully. "Lucky for me that your backpack's so . . . bright. I might not have spotted you otherwise. I've never seen one like it."

"I made it." Wendy shrugged. "I made the pack, anyway. I bought the frame from a mail-order house."

"Ah," I said, rubbing my hands together for warmth, "a hard-core hiker. Are you doing one of the long-distance trails?" I'd learned from Emma's map collection that England was crisscrossed by a trail system that made it possible to walk the entire length and breadth of the island.

"I was, until I got turned around." Wendy opened the door nearest the Victorian range, poked her head inside, and pulled a small flashlight from her pocket, murmuring, "The twenty-first century intrudes."

"Does it?" I asked.

"Come and see," she said, and stepped

through the doorway.

I joined her in what turned out to be a second kitchen. It was much smaller than the one we'd left, and its furnishings were distinctly non-Victorian. Wendy's flashlight revealed sleek teak cabinetry, polished granite countertops, two microwaves, a marble-topped island, a stainless-steel refrigerator, floor-to-ceiling steel shelves filled with small appliances, and a butter-yellow Aga gas oven.

"I'll bet this is where they do the real cooking," I said. "They must have preserved the other kitchen as a sort of historical showpiece."

Wendy moved along the counters, opening one cabinet after another, then peered into the refrigerator.

"If this is where they do the real cooking, then they must be on a strict diet," she commented, "because the cupboards are bare." She sighed and raised a gloved hand to warm her nose. "I don't know about you, but I could use a cup of tea."

"I'd settle for a cup of hot water," I said, and touched the Aga cooker. It was cold. "The gas must be turned off. And the microwaves won't work because the electricity is out."

"Looks like we'll have to rely on historical technology," Wendy said as she headed back into the big kitchen.

I trotted after her, asking, "Are you going to try the range? It looks like it's a hundred years old. Do you know how it works?"

"Not yet." Wendy lifted an empty coal scuttle from the whitewashed hearth, pointed to an oversized teakettle sitting on the range, and strode toward the darkened corridor. "You fill the kettle, I'll find the coal."

I did as I was told, humbled by her air of confident competence. The complicated range overawed me, but I was pretty sure I could handle a pair of spigots.

I was still filling the kettle when Wendy returned with a full scuttle and began shoveling coal into the range's vintage gullet.

"The coal hole's next to the boiler room," she told me. "The corridor's lined with service rooms and leads to the main part of the house. I don't think anyone's here but us."

I agreed. Since the Aga was cold, the kitchen freezing, and the hot running water nonexistent, I suspected that Ladythorne's owner was not currently in residence. I turned the water off, hauled the heavy kettle to the range, and watched while Wendy fiddled with tinder, flues, and matches. In no time at all, the range began to give off a faint whisper of blessed warmth.

"I am more impressed than I can possibly say," I declared, holding my hands over the range.

Wendy glanced at my lightweight down jacket. "You're a little underdressed for the weather, aren't you?"

"I wasn't expecting to run into a blizzard," I said. "No one was. There wasn't a hint of it in the weather forecasts."

"It's a tricky time of year," Wendy commented. "It pays to be prepared for anything."

I gave her a sidelong look. "Is that why you carry a pry bar? I mean, most backpackers settle for a Swiss Army knife."

"I've been remodeling my house for the past few years." Wendy moved to the white dresser and began rummaging through the drawers and the enclosed lower shelves. "I've gotten used to having certain tools handy. The pry bar's good for splitting wood."

And for housebreaking. The thought popped into my head so unexpectedly that

I didn't know where to look. I fixed my gaze resolutely on the teakettle, then let it sidle furtively to the red backpack.

A slender tendril of suspicion was taking root in my mind. It suddenly struck me as odd that an experienced hiker should choose such a tricky time of year to ramble through England; odder still that a lone American armed with a pry bar should happen upon such an out-of-the-way corner of the Cotswolds. I'd never laid eyes on Ladythorne Abbey before, and I lived only twenty — or so — miles away from it. And try as I might, I couldn't for the life of me remember seeing a long-distance trail on Emma's map of the valley.

As my gaze drifted back to the teakettle, I was assailed by yet another disquieting thought — I was almost certain that Wendy couldn't have tried the front door before slipping around to the back. The snow on the front stairs had been undisturbed, and there'd been no tracks leading from them to the cloister. Why, I wondered, would Wendy lie to me? More important: Why would she sneak into the house through the back door instead of presenting herself at the front?

The disturbing questions provoked disturbing answers. I'd heard of burglars making hit-and-run raids on unoccupied country houses, and Ladythorne Abbey's splendid isolation made it seem particularly vulnerable. A clever burglar might park a car some distance away from the house and hike in, disguised as an innocent backpacker, to see if the place was worth plundering. I looked at Wendy and felt a chill despite the range's increasing heat. Was she a clever burglar? I wondered. Had I stumbled onto a crime-in-progress?

"You know what?" I said brightly. "I should call my husband. I should let him know that I'm alive and kicking. To tell the truth, I'm kind of surprised he hasn't phoned me. The last time I got lost in bad weather he called out the army to find me."

"The army?" Wendy straightened abruptly and gave me a sharp look. "Are you joking?"

"I'm absolutely serious," I said. "I was caught in a deluge up in Northumberland and —"

"There's no phone here," Wendy interrupted, frowning. "At least, there're no lines running to the house. I checked."

"You checked?" I echoed, raising an eyebrow.

Wendy dropped her gaze. "It's . . . a bad

storm. I thought I might need to call for help."

I whistled softly. "You must've been one heck of a Girl Scout, Wendy. It never crossed my mind to check for phone lines, but maybe that's because I brought a cell phone with me. You're welcome to use it."

Wendy's worried frown eased. "No, thanks. I don't need to call anyone. But you go ahead and call your husband. Make sure he knows that you're okay. The army has better things to do than to rescue us." She resumed her search of the dresser. "I'll see if I can find some tea leaves and maybe a bite to eat."

"I've got food," I told her. "We can divvy it up when I finish my phone call."

I retrieved the cell phone from my day pack and stepped into the corridor, pondering Wendy's shifting moods. She'd seemed perturbed by my mention of the army, and relieved to know that I could head them off with a reassuring word in Bill's ear. I couldn't imagine why she'd object to being rescued, but I could think of at least one reason why she might not want to face the army — or anyone else in authority. Burglars, as a rule, are not fond of men in uniform.

It wasn't until I stood in the gloomy corridor that I realized why Bill hadn't called me. I'd evidently been so sleepy-headed when Emma had picked me up that I'd forgotten to turn the cell phone on. I quickly corrected my error and speed-dialed my home number. Bill answered on the first ring.

"Lori?"

"Yep, it's me," I said, "and I'm okay."

"I've been trying to call you —"

"Sorry," I broke in. "The phone was switched off."

"Where are you?" Bill demanded.

"Ladythorne Abbey," I replied. "You should have no trouble finding it. It's on Emma's map, but it's not a ruin, it's a big old house with a roof and walls and —"

"I know the place," said Bill.

I stared at the phone for a moment, dumbfounded, then put it back to my ear and asked, "How?"

"A client purchased it and its contents a couple of years ago," Bill told me. "I advised against it — the house was in terrible shape — but she was adamant. She insisted that no price was too high to pay for the kind of privacy Ladythorne offered. I'm glad to hear it has a roof."

"So am I," I said with heartfelt sincerity, "but I'd still rather be under my own. How soon can you come get me?"

Bill sighed. "Not sure, love. We're completely snowed in here, and it's still coming down. I can't even open the garage door."

"Try a pry bar," I suggested. "That's how we got in here."

"What?" Bill exclaimed. "What pry bar? And who's *we?*"

"I ran into another hiker," I told him, "the self-reliant kind. Comes with her own housebreaking equipment."

"Lori . . ." Bill said warily.

"I'm not making it up," I retorted. "Her name is Wendy Walker. She's from Long Island, she carries a pry bar in her backpack, and I think she may have told me a few big fat lies. Bill," I continued, lowering my voice, "have you heard of any burglaries in the area recently?"

"Not recently," said Bill, "and certainly none pulled off by someone on foot, if that's what you're suggesting. The preferred method is to drive a moving van up to the front door, clear a place out, and make a run for it. Your backpacker would have a tough time making a fast getaway, and if she spent the night anywhere near the scene of the crime, she'd be a prime suspect."

Bill's argument made a certain amount

of sense, but I wasn't willing to abandon my theory so easily. "What if she disguised herself as a backpacker so she could check out the house for the guys with the moving van?"

"She wouldn't carry a big backpack," Bill answered. "Why weigh herself down when she could pretend to be a casual walker, like you?"

"But she says she's walking one of the long-distance trails," I countered, "and there aren't any long-distance trails on Emma's map."

"Are you sure?" Bill asked. It was a loaded question. My husband knew that map-reading wasn't among my most polished skills.

"I'm *pretty* sure. Okay," I conceded, "I may have misread the map, but what about the missing footprints?" I could almost see Bill rolling his eyes while I explained why I believed that Wendy couldn't have approached the front door before slinking around to the back.

"Lori," he said patiently, when I'd finished, "it's snowing out. It's snowing very heavily. Is it possible that Wendy's tracks filled with snow before you had a chance to spot them? Is it possible that the wind was blowing so hard that you couldn't see anything clearly?"

"It's possible," I allowed, and grudgingly reconsidered my position. Perhaps I had read too much into the situation. It wouldn't be the first time my imagination had run away with me.

"Lori," Bill said, "do you truly believe that this Wendy Walker is a criminal?"

"I guess not," I said reluctantly. "The pry bar spooked me, that's all. She says she uses it for splitting wood."

"Sounds reasonable," said Bill. "Diehard campers carry lots of weird tools. How are you for food?"

"I've got Emma's picnic lunch," I reminded him. "If we need more, I expect Wendy'll go out and shoot a moose or something."

Bill's chuckle held an endearingly vibrant note of relief. "It's good to hear your voice."

"Likewise," I said. "But we mustn't overindulge. Since I don't know how long I'm going to be here, I should probably conserve the phone's battery. I'll call again at five, okay?"

"I'll be waiting. There's not much else I can do." Bill paused before adding, "Listen, love, if you're worried about Wendy —"

"I'm not," I assured him. "It's just my frostbitten brain running amok."

"Okay," said Bill. "If you're sure . . ."

"I'm sure," I said. "Kiss the boys for me." As I ended the call, I noted the time on the cell phone's backlit screen. It was ten past one. Less than two hours had passed since the blizzard had struck. It had felt like an eternity.

The table was set when I returned to the kitchen. In rummaging through the dresser, Wendy had produced cups, saucers, plates, cutlery, a pair of much-mended linen napkins, and an eight-cup brown earthenware teapot. She'd also found the tea tin and the sugar canister, both of which were, thankfully, full.

"Is your husband coming to get you?" she asked.

"Eventually," I replied. "At the moment he's as stuck as we are. If you ask me, every weatherman in this country will be looking for a new job tomorrow morning."

I took off my gloves and shoved them in my pockets, opened my day pack, and unloaded the picnic lunch. Emma must have expected the fresh air to sharpen my appetite because she'd packed four chicken-and-watercress sandwiches, a large wedge of Stilton cheese, two crusty baguettes, two apples, a half dozen chocolate bars, and four enormous cranberry muffins.

Wendy expressed her admiration of the feast before adding, with a touch of sarcasm, "Cute bunny. I'll bet he's helpful in emergencies."

I looked at the table and realized that I'd unpacked Reginald along with the picnic lunch. He was sitting between the wedge of Stilton and the apples, holding his paws out to the range.

I felt my face redden. "He's a . . . a mascot. A lucky charm."

"Not so lucky today," Wendy observed.

"Oh, I don't know," I said, tucking Reginald back into the day pack. "I think I was pretty lucky to find my way here. It beats camping out in a snowdrift."

While we waited for the water to boil, Wendy munched on an apple and treated me to a guided tour of the Victorian range. She pointed out the plate-warming rack, the open grill, the roasting spits, the multiple ovens, the warming compartments, and the complicated flues.

"That's a reservoir," she concluded, touching a spigot that protruded from a flat panel covering the lower-right quarter of the range. "It's designed to heat large quantities of water. I filled it while you were on the phone and it seems to be working pretty efficiently."

The range was, in fact, churning out the kind of heat that would make summer bread-baking a misery. I put my stocking cap in the day pack and hung my jacket on the back of a chair. When Wendy took off her own jacket, I saw that beneath the bulky parka lurked a slender woman with broad shoulders and an enviably slim waistline. She wore what appeared to be a hand-knit wool sweater in shades of gray that went well with her blue-gray eyes. When I complimented her on the sweater, she told me she'd knitted it herself.

"Do you have one of these monsters at home?" I asked, nodding toward the range.

"I have a microwave," she conceded. "But I've read about ranges, and I enjoy figuring out how things work."

"What are you?" I joked. "A rocket scientist?"

"Yes," she replied.

I studied her perfectly straight face and decided that she must be telling the truth.

"I work for a company that monitors orbiting satellites," she amended, with a small smile.

"That would explain why you can work a

coal stove." I ran my fingers through my stocking cap–crushed curls. "Is February a slow month in the satellite business? I can't think of any other reason to hike a long-distance trail in England at this time of year."

"It's the perfect time of year for hiking," Wendy countered. "Air fares and hotels are dirt cheap, and the trails are virtually empty. I like saving money, and I like having the trails to myself."

I eyed her curiously. "Have you been staying in hotels?"

"I have so far," said Wendy. "As I said, they're dirt cheap."

I was about to ask why, if she was staying in hotels, she found it necessary to split wood, when the kettle let out a shriek and we busied ourselves with the all-important task of brewing a lifesaving pot of tea. I'd just deposited the steaming teapot on the table when the door to the courtyard flew open with a bang.

"What the . . ." I began, and sputtered into silence as yet another backpacker marched into the kitchen, followed closely by an old man with a shotgun.

"Thieves!" the old man bellowed before turning to point the shotgun straight at me.

Four

My heart skipped a beat. My mind went blank. Though my feet had finally thawed, I stood frozen in place. No one had ever pointed a gun at me before. It was a novel experience I hoped never to repeat.

"Uh . . ." I quavered before lapsing into stupefied silence.

Wendy's nerves, by contrast, were evidently made of stainless steel.

"Would you please point that thing somewhere else?" she asked the intruder. "And please close the door. You're letting the heat escape."

"Don't you be giving me orders, missy," the old man growled. He was seventy if he was a day, unshaven and wild-eyed, clad in scuffed hobnailed boots, a half dozen woolly scarves, and a tattered canvas jacket any self-respecting charity shop would have rejected. The shotgun, on the other hand, was immaculate.

"She said 'please,' " the old man's captive pointed out. "Twice."

"You keep your mouth shut," the old man barked, but he kicked the door shut and swung the shotgun away from me to its original position, nudging his hostage further into the room.

The hostage wore faded jeans, a blue parka, and hiking boots. He was male, tall, slender, and — at a guess — somewhere in his late thirties. Snow clung to his forest-green backpack and to the tangle of dark curls spilling from his stocking cap nearly to his shoulders. The dark beard and mustache encircling his lips looked as soft as eiderdown, and his chestnut-brown eyes betrayed not a trace of fear.

"Forgive me," he said quietly. "I didn't mean to speak out of turn. May I remove my backpack? Please? It's been rather a long day."

"Go ahead." The old man poked the backpack viciously with the shotgun. "But if you make one false move, I'll blow your thieving head off!"

The old man's brutal response to the backpacker's humble request roused my most protective maternal instincts. As the dark-haired man removed his heavy pack and set it carefully on the floor, my terror was abruptly overwhelmed by fury.

"Y-you bully!" I shouted, freed from my

fear-induced paralysis. "If you want to shoot someone, shoot me, because frankly, given a choice between being held prisoner by a trigger-happy lunatic and having my head blown off, I'd sooner have my head blown off. So go ahead, Mr. Big Shot, *pull the trigger!*"

The old man glanced at me uncertainly, as if he thought *I* might be a lunatic, and in that moment of uncertainty the younger man ducked, twisted, and swung around in one graceful movement, grasping the shotgun by both barrels and removing it deftly from the older man's grip. The old man flailed at him briefly, then shrank back against the door and folded his arms. He seemed more disgruntled than cowed.

The dark-haired man stepped back, broke the shotgun, and peered into the breech. His lips twitched in an amused smile as he looked from the gun to the old man. "How, may I ask, were you planning to blow my head off? You've forgotten to load your weapon."

"Didn't forget," the old man retorted. "Don't believe in wasting good shot on vermin."

"I can assume that you don't happen to have any shells in your pockets, then? Good. It was unkind of you to frighten the ladies. We wouldn't want it to happen again." The dark-haired man placed the shotgun on the white dresser's highest shelf, well out of the older man's reach, and motioned toward the table. "Now we can have a civilized conversation. Won't you sit down, Mr. . . . ?"

"Catchpole," snapped the old man. "No Mister. Just Catchpole." He scowled at his former prisoner, but took a seat at the table. "And what would your name be, sonny? I'm sure the coppers'll want to know, if they don't already."

"I'm Jamie Macrae. No Mister. Just Jamie." The name was Scottish, but the accent was an odd blend of midwestern American and upper-class English.

"A filthy Yank," muttered Catchpole. "A filthy, thieving Yank come to strip the abbey bare. Dear Lord, what would Miss DeClerke say?"

"You're American?" I said to Jamie. "So are we. I'm Lori Shepherd, and this is Wendy Walker."

"Pleased to meet you." Jamie Macrae piled his cap, gloves, and parka on his backpack, brushed snow from the collar of his bulky, dark-blue turtleneck, and sat at the table, with his back to the dresser, as if determined to keep himself between

Catchpole and the shotgun. "Can you spare a cup of tea, by any chance? It's a bit blustery out there."

"We noticed," Wendy said dryly. She fetched two more cups and saucers from the dresser and poured tea for everyone, including Catchpole.

The old man was holding his head between his hands and muttering to himself. "*Three* Yanks? Dear Lord in heaven, what would Miss DeClerke say if she knew that three lying, thieving Yanks —"

"How do we know *you're* not a thief?" Wendy broke in, taking a seat directly across from the old man.

"A thief?" Catchpole raised his grizzled head to glare at her. "I'm Catchpole, the caretaker," he barked. "I've worked at Ladythorne my whole life. It's my job to look after the abbey and I'll be damned" — he thumped the table with a fist — "if I'll let a mob of gangsters ransack it!"

"Oh, for pity's sake," I said impatiently. "Do we look like gangsters? We're here because of the blizzard. I don't know if you've noticed, but it's coming down in buckets out there, and this is the only shelter for miles."

Catchpole jutted his chin toward Jamie. "I suppose himself there was looking for shelter in the family vaults?"

"As a matter of fact, I was," Jamie said mildly. "I didn't realize there was a house until you marched me up to it. I'm glad you did. I wasn't looking forward to camping out in a mausoleum."

The old man gazed sourly from Jamie's face to mine. "Are you telling me that *three Yanks* came to the *abbey* in *February* by *accident?*"

If I'd been honest, I'd have admitted to Catchpole that I shared his incredulity. The odds against three Americans washing up on such a remote shore in England's least trustworthy month struck me as very long indeed. I didn't want to set the old man off again, however, so I simply nodded and said earnestly, "I promise you, Mr. — er — Catchpole, I didn't come here to steal anything, and I'll gladly reimburse Miss DeClerke for the coal and the tea and whatever else we might have to use while we're here. I'll pay for the broken lock as well," I added, with a quick glance at Wendy. "And I'll apologize to Miss DeClerke for any inconvenience we may cause her."

Catchpole gave a grim chuckle. "You'll have a hard time doing that, missy."

"Why?" I asked.

"Because Miss DeClerke is *dead.*" Catchpole regarded me with gloomy triumph. "Miss Gibbs owns the abbey now. It's her coal you're thieving, her you'll have to answer to, and she's a rich lady, is Miss Gibbs. She's not one to be trifled with."

"Miss Gibbs?" I stared at him open-mouthed, then sank into the chair next to his. "You don't mean Tessa Gibbs, do you? The actress?"

"That's the one," said Catchpole. "She bought Ladythorne two years ago, closed the deal a month before Miss DeClerke died, and when she finds out —"

"But I know her!" I exclaimed. "I know Tessa Gibbs. That is, my husband does. He's an attorney. Tessa's one of his clients. He told me that one of his clients had bought Ladythorne, but he didn't tell me her name."

"Pull the other one," Catchpole grunted. "It's got bells on."

"He stayed at Tessa's chalet in Lucerne," I said, determined to convince the old man that I was telling the truth. "He told me about it. Tessa has a personal assistant, Liz something-or-other, and her masseuse is from Helsinki."

Catchpole sniffed. "Could've read about them in any fan magazine."

I searched my memory for other, more arcane tidbits Bill had let fall about the world-famous film star. "Tessa's cook is named Rhadu."

"Rhadu?" echoed Wendy, doubtfully.

"She's Hindu," I explained. "Tessa's a vegetarian, except . . ."

Catchpole's gaze slid to my face.

"Except for pork scratchings," I finished. "She loved them as a child, apparently, and can't shake the habit. It's her dirty little secret. She told Bill that if word ever gets out that she binges on something as totally nonvegetarian as pork scratchings, she'll lose credibility with —"

"No one knows about the pork scratchings," Catchpole interrupted irritably. "Who told you about the pork scratchings?"

"My husband." Exasperated, I dragged my day pack across the table, pulled the cell phone from the outer pocket, and presented it to the obstinate old man. "Here. Call him. His name is Bill Willis. He'll back me up."

Catchpole eyed the cell phone nervously. "Your husband's an attorney, is he?"

"He's a well-known and extremely powerful attorney," I replied, carefully emphasizing the adjectives. "After he's answered any questions you might have about me, I'm sure he'll be able to fill you in on the gun laws in this country. I believe they're rather strict, aren't they, Jamie?"

"So I've heard," Jamie agreed.

"Especially concerning guns pointed at people," added Wendy helpfully.

The old caretaker looked from one implacable face to the next, then cleared his throat, and waved the cell phone aside. "No need to ring your husband, madam. I'm sure Miss Gibbs won't mind if her attorney's wife visits the abbey. It's my belief, in fact, that she'll be well pleased to know that you found shelter here, you and your chums. I apologize for the misunderstanding and hope you won't trouble your husband about it. And don't worry your head about the broken lock. I'll take care of it." He pushed his chair back from the table. "Now, then, who'd like milk in their tea?"

We all wanted milk in our tea, and Catchpole obligingly went up the corridor to fetch it. We three Yanks remained silent until he'd shut the door behind him.

"Do you suppose he's gone to find another gun?" I asked, returning the cell phone to my day pack. "He's certainly got a bee in his bonnet about Americans."

"I wouldn't worry about another gun," said Wendy. "You've graduated from 'missy' to 'madam.' He's on our side, now. Your powerful attorney husband did the trick."

"No, no," said Jamie, shaking his head solemnly. "I'm sure it was the pork scratchings."

A current of relief ran through our muted laughter. I couldn't be sure about the others, but I felt as if I'd sought shelter in a cave only to find it occupied by a ferocious, Yank-eating lion. I considered myself fortunate to have emerged from the encounter unscathed.

"That was a pretty slick move you pulled on the old man," I said, gazing admiringly at Jamie. "It was brave, too. You couldn't've known that the shotgun was unloaded."

"It's experience rather than bravery," said Jamie, deflecting the compliment. "I've run into men like Catchpole before. Their bark is nearly always worse than their bite."

"Still . . . thanks." I was curious to know more about my brave compatriot, but I was also becoming slightly lightheaded from hunger. Smiling, I offered him a sandwich and said, "Eat up. If you've been slogging through snowdrifts, you must be ravenous."

"I am a bit peckish," he admitted.

"Then dig in," I said, and the long-delayed picnic lunch began.

Emma's lunch, though ample for one person, proved to be less so for three. We went through it like a swarm of locusts, leaving only a pair of well-gnawed apple cores in our wake. While Jamie and Wendy finished the cranberry muffins, I ate the last of the chocolate bars and daydreamed of roast suckling pig. I was so absorbed in my culinary fantasy that I didn't bother to look up when Catchpole returned.

"Sorry to be so long, madam," he said, directing his words to me, "but I thought you might want something warm in your belly, so I brought a few bits and bobs to heat through."

I came out of my reverie as Catchpole approached the oak table, pushing a butler's cart piled high with cans, bottles, and sealed packets. I peered at the assembled foods in wonder, taken aback by the old man's largesse.

"Is that" — I licked my lips — "lobster bisque?"

"That's right, madam," confirmed

Catchpole. "Lobster bisque, asparagus spears with truffle sauce, risotto with sun-dried tomatoes, dried chanterelle mushrooms, and smoked mussels. I can use the macaroons and the tinned fruit to make a pudding. Oh, and here's some long-shelf-life milk for your tea." He placed the carton on the table, adding, "There's plenty more where that came from. Miss Gibbs keeps a full larder for her guests."

"God bless Miss Gibbs," I said fervently, and promptly accepted Catchpole's offer to prepare a hot meal for me and my chums.

Catchpole completed his stunning transformation from cantankerous curmudgeon to obsequious servant by removing his patched canvas jacket and collection of tattered scarves and revealing a set of garments that weren't nearly as disreputable as I'd expected. The argyle sweater-vest might not have been the best choice to go with the plaid flannel shirt, but both were clean and tidy, and the corduroy trousers were spotless.

"It's a good thing Miss Gibbs keeps so much food on hand," said Catchpole as he reached for a saucepan. "Looks like you'll need it, madam."

"What do you mean?" I asked, wondering if by some miracle I looked underfed.

"I mean that you'll be spending at least one night here, madam, and probably more," said Catchpole. "Snow's halfway up the doors already and shows no sign of stopping. It'll be two days or more, I reckon, before the big plows reach the abbey."

Wendy, Jamie, and I rose as one and crossed to look out the Gothic windows. Catchpole was right. The snowdrifts were piled to the sills and getting deeper by the minute.

I groaned softly. "We'll be lucky to get out of here by May."

"We're lucky to be here in the first place," Wendy reminded me. "Imagine what would've happened if we'd been caught —"

"Don't." I shuddered and wrapped my arms around myself. I could imagine it much too vividly.

"Let's focus on counting our blessings," Jamie suggested, putting a comforting hand on my shoulder. "We've got food and shelter, warmth and companionship. What more could we ask?"

"A change of underwear would be nice," I muttered. I turned to gesture toward the backpacks. "You guys came prepared for camping out. I came prepared for a stroll. I was supposed to sleep at home tonight, in my own jammies, in my own warm bed. I don't even have a change of socks."

Catchpole evidently overheard my plaintive grumbling because he called over his shoulder, "Don't worry your head about clothes, madam. Miss Gibbs keeps spares on hand for her guests. And the guest rooms are finished up proper. I'll show 'em to you after you've eaten."

"Ask and you shall receive," Jamie murmured.

"Amen," I murmured back.

While Jamie and Wendy rinsed the dishes from our first meal, I set the table for our second. The bisque's spicy aroma wafted through the kitchen as Catchpole turned his attention to the simmering risotto.

"Catchpole," I said, returning to my chair, "if Miss Gibbs entertains so often, why hasn't she installed phones? And why isn't there any hot water? And why —"

"She hasn't entertained anyone yet, madam," Catchpole interrupted. "She's getting ready, you might say. Miss DeClerke let the abbey run down a bit before she died, you see, and Miss Gibbs has spent the past two years fixing it up. It's been a big job, though, restoring the electric, laying on the gas, replacing old pipes, fixing the roof, making a kitchen Miss Rhadu won't spit at and guest rooms fit for guests. Miss Gibbs's got a big affair planned for April — the unveiling, she calls it — and we're hoping everything'll be finished by then. But for now it's oil lamps for light, and fires in the grates for warmth."

"Do you live in the abbey?" I asked.

"No, madam, I've a cottage out back, not too far from the family vaults." Catchpole glanced at Jamie. "That's how I spotted Mr. Macrae, creeping about."

Jamie was still at the sink with Wendy, but he turned at the mention of his name. "It's hard to do anything *but* creep in knee-deep snow."

Catchpole shook a wooden spoon at him. "You didn't half give me a turn, young man. Thought you were a DeClerke, risen from the grave. Not but what Miss DeClerke'll be spinning in hers, knowing three Yanks have invaded the abbey. Won't be a bit surprised if she comes back to cut your throats in the night."

My hand went involuntarily to my own throat.

"What a grisly thing to say," Wendy commented. "Especially after a meal."

"You're talking nonsense, Catchpole." Jamie came to stand by my side. "You don't really believe in ghosts, do you?"

Catchpole lowered the spoon and met Jamie's level gaze with one of his own.

"I believe in hatred," he said. "And if hatred can bring a soul back from the grave, then you'd best keep a lookout for Miss DeClerke tonight. If I were you, I'd sleep with one eye open."

For a moment the only sound in the kitchen was the *plop-plop* of the simmering risotto. I saw Jamie glance uncertainly at Wendy, who stood frozen at the sink, plate in hand, staring hard at the caretaker. Their silence surprised me. Instead of scoffing at Catchpole for being a superstitious fool, they seemed to be taking him seriously.

I didn't. I thought the old humbug was trying to scare us again, and I refused to let him get away with it.

"Thanks a lot, Catchpole," I said, my voice laden with disgust. "The blizzard and the shotgun weren't bad enough? Now you have to add a knife-wielding ghost to our evening's entertainment? When my husband hears about this —"

"I was only joking, madam," Catchpole said hastily. He managed a nervous grin. "Some folk enjoy a good ghost story."

Wendy sighed softly. "I think we've had enough chills for one day."

"More than enough." Jamie's face had gone pale despite his windburn.

"We don't need anymore," I stated firmly. "So keep your spooky stories to yourself, please. Although . . ." I glanced diffidently at the others. "I wouldn't mind hearing more about Miss DeClerke — the real Miss DeClerke, not the alleged ghost. She sounds fascinating. Why did she hate Americans so much?"

"Because she was kind to 'em, madam," Catchpole replied. "She was kind to 'em, and they betrayed her."

Five

The lobster bisque was exquisite, the risotto superb, but the true highlight of the meal was the tale that accompanied it. As the food disappeared and dusk began to settle, Catchpole joined us at the table and told us what he knew about the mysteriously vindictive Miss DeClerke. He spoke so eagerly and at such length that I felt a touch of pity for him. As the caretaker of a remote country estate, he probably didn't have many opportunities for social interaction. His garrulity seemed to me to be a wistful by-product of loneliness.

"What you have to understand right off is that, despite what I said earlier, I haven't always lived at the abbey," he began. "When Dad was called up, Mother and I went to live with her people in Shropshire. That was in September, nineteen forty. We didn't come back till 'forty-six, so some of what I know I learned secondhand, after everything had gone to pieces.

"It was the war that did it," he went on.

"Miss DeClerke was only seventeen when it started, and engaged to a viscount's son. Her father was over the moon about the marriage. His wife had died years before and Miss DeClerke was his only child; his only living relative, in truth — the last of the line. He'd hoped she'd make a good match, and she did him proud. What's more, she loved the lad, and he loved her."

"How did Miss DeClerke's mother die?" Wendy asked.

"Influenza epidemic, after the Great War," said Catchpole. "Swept away millions."

"Influenza." Wendy pushed her soup bowl aside and stared down at her risotto. "Sorry to interrupt. You were telling us about Miss DeClerke's marriage."

"The marriage that never was," said Catchpole. "Everything was arranged for a June wedding — dress made, invitations sent, the London house decked out for the reception — but it never happened. Miss DeClerke's young man joined his regiment when war was declared, you see. He sailed off with the expeditionary force and died of wounds received during the evacuation of Dunkirk. That was in May."

"The end of May," Jamie murmured, laying his spoon on the table.

"Yes, sir," said Catchpole. "He died on the twenty-ninth of May, nineteen forty. I was only six years old when it happened, but I remember the day Miss DeClerke came back from London. Dressed in black, she was, and looking as if a falling leaf might knock her over. My mother sent me after her when she went walking in the woods, to watch over her, like, and make sure she didn't do herself a mischief. Miss DeClerke didn't seem to mind." Catchpole caught my eye. "You may find it hard to believe, madam, but I didn't talk much as a child. I believe that's why Miss DeClerke let me tag along." He pushed his chair back from the table and rose. "If you'll excuse me, madam, I'll fetch the oil lamps from the lamp room. We'll be needing 'em shortly."

"I'll come with you," Wendy offered. "I've always wanted to see a lamp room."

"It's through here, ma'am." Catchpole directed Wendy into the darkened corridor, leaving Jamie and me alone in the kitchen.

We'd finished the main meal. All that remained was the baked apricot compote Catchpole had prepared for dessert. While Jamie spooned the bubbling compote into bowls to cool, I washed the dinner dishes and scoured the pots and pans, leaving them to dry in the wooden rack.

"One more," said Jamie, crossing to hand me the saucepan he'd emptied.

I scrubbed it clean and placed it in the rack, but remained at the sink, peering out the windows. The courtyard was unrecognizable. The outbuildings looked like white hillocks in an arctic desert, and although the wind had slackened, snow continued to tumble from the cloud-crowded sky. I felt cut off from the world, marooned in a landscape as alien as that of the moon.

"Hard to believe it's only half past three," I said. "It's getting dark already."

"It's the clouds. They've swallowed the sun." Jamie leaned back against the sink and asked, "Are you all right? You sound . . . melancholy."

I sighed. "Influenza epidemic, canceled wedding, dead fiancé, war — it's a sad story."

"It may become sadder," Jamie cautioned. "We haven't heard the rest of it yet. Would you like me to ask Catchpole to stop?"

"No, I wouldn't." I glanced toward the corridor and lowered my voice. "He hasn't gotten to the part about the Americans yet."

Jamie leaned forward, his elbows resting on the sink. "I wonder how they fit in? Miss DeClerke couldn't blame them for Dunkirk, surely."

"You never know," I told him. "She was young and heartbroken. Maybe she needed to blame someone, and it didn't much matter who. But we don't have to guess. Catchpole will tell us."

"Are you sure you want him to?" said Jamie.

"Positive." I peered at him questioningly. "Don't you?"

"Of course." Jamie straightened and regarded me steadily. "So long as he doesn't upset you."

I was tempted to remind my chivalrous protector that he'd gone pale at the mention of Miss DeClerke's homicidal ghost while I hadn't turned a hair, and that if anyone needed reassurance, it was him, but I was so touched by his kindness that I smiled instead.

"There's no need to worry about me," I said. "I'm tough as old boots. I have to be — my sons discovered slugs last summer."

Jamie laughed and was about to speak when Wendy and Catchpole emerged from the corridor carrying four tall, old-fashioned glass oil lamps. The lamps' neatly trimmed wicks burned steadily, casting a golden glow over the old oak table and the bowls of glistening apricots, but shadows filled the corners of the room and crept along the ceiling's vaulted ribs. It was comforting to move away from the frosty windows and into the warm circle of light.

The compote was comforting, too, warm and sweet, with precisely the right amount of tartness. I dug into my share with pleasure while Catchpole carried on as if there'd been no interruption.

"The first of the great bombing raids hit London in September," he said. "My dad was called up then. He was in his forties, too old to be going to war, but England expected every man to do his duty, so off he went. And Mother and I went to Shropshire. She felt bad about leaving, Mother did, but with the able-bodied men gone from the farm, her family needed her. Miss DeClerke chose to stay on at the abbey. She was here when she got the news that her father had been killed."

"Killed?" Wendy said, her dessert spoon frozen in midair. "How?"

"A bombing raid," Catchpole replied. "He'd gone down to the London house, to take care of some trifling business. He was supposed to stay only the one night, but he never came back. It was a full-moon night, you see, the kind of night Adolph's boys liked best. The London house was demolished, burnt to the ground, not a stone left standing. That was in October."

"I'd no idea," Jamie murmured. "The October raids were brutal, but I'd no idea. . . ." He shook his head and looked around the room, as if seeing it for the first time. "Ladythorne seems so tranquil, so removed from the outside world, yet the war left its scars, even here."

"The war scarred all of us, sir, one way or another," said Catchpole. "My dad came home safe, thank the Lord, but I lost two uncles and whole raft of cousins. Miss DeClerke, poor soul, lost everyone she held dear — her father and her fiancé. She had more money than she knew what to do with, but what good was it to her? She'd lost what she truly treasured."

"What did she do?" I asked. "Did she leave the abbey?"

"You'd expect it of her, wouldn't you, madam?" said Catchpole. "A young girl alone in this great rambling house, with only a handful of servants to keep her company, and them too old or daft to be of much use. You'd expect her to shut the place up and run away, wouldn't you?"

I reached for my cup of tea. "It would have been tempting."

"Not for her, it wasn't." Catchpole planted his elbows on the table and clasped his hands together. "Miss DeClerke stayed put and fought back the only way she knew how. That young slip of a girl turned the abbey into a convalescent home, where officers could come to recover from their injuries. The army may have staffed the place, but she ran it, and she made sure her officers had the best of everything."

"Must've been difficult, with rationing," Jamie commented.

"Had a victory garden, didn't she? Raised chickens and pigs, kept a few milk cows. Miss DeClerke never let rationing bother her." A reminiscent smile played on the old man's lips. "Her officers had the run of the house — billiards room, library, music room, long gallery. They sat out in the cloisters when the weather was fine, used the tennis courts if they were able, slept on linen sheets, ate off the finest china."

"She found a good use for her money," I observed.

"She found a good use for her heart," Catchpole countered. He frowned down at the table before adding gruffly, "Every officer reminded her of her young man, you see. She couldn't do enough for 'em."

I glanced at the shotgun lying on the dresser's topmost shelf. The twin barrels gleamed softly in the lamplight. "Were they British officers?"

"They were, at first." Catchpole's frown deepened. "But as the war was winding down, they started sending Americans. I don't know why — you'd think they'd look after their own — but whatever the reason, they came. By the end of the war it was nothing but Yanks, but Miss DeClerke didn't mind. She welcomed 'em with open arms, treated 'em the same as her British gentlemen — until they stabbed her in the back."

"What did they do?" I asked, on tenterhooks.

"I don't know." Sparks of rage lit Catchpole's eyes. "But whatever it was, it drove Miss DeClerke mad."

If anticlimaxes could kill, I would have been stretched out stone-cold on the black-and-white tiles. I felt as if *I'd* been stabbed in the back — I'd listened faithfully to an hour's worth of buildup and I *still* didn't know why Miss DeClerke hated Americans. I dug my spoon savagely into the remnants of my cooling compote while Wendy and Jamie exchanged looks of disbelief. Disappointment had rendered each of us momentarily speechless.

"Y-you don't know?" I managed. "You burst in here waving a gun and screaming insults about Yanks and *you don't know why?*"

"I don't know *exactly* what happened," Catchpole admitted grudgingly. "I only know that Miss DeClerke reported it to the authorities, and they told her not to make a fuss. It was the end of the war, you see, and they didn't want a scandal ruffling allied feathers. There was a big enough mess to clear up, they told her, without having an hysterical Englishwoman accusing American soldiers of misbehavior."

"But you don't know what *kind* of misbehavior," I said peevishly.

Catchpole had the grace to look vaguely shamefaced. "Miss DeClerke never spoke of it, and the servants who were here when it happened were either dead of old age by the time Mother and Dad brought me back, or too daft to understand what the fuss had been about."

Wendy leaned her chin on her hand. "Did Miss DeClerke hire new servants?"

"Yes, but they didn't stay long. Miss

DeClerke had gone a bit . . . peculiar . . . by then." Catchpole cleared his throat uncomfortably. "She wouldn't let Yanks set foot on her property, wouldn't use anything American-made, sacked anyone who so much as mentioned your country in passing. She'd taken to spending a good deal of time in her room, too, writing letters and posting them off to America."

"To America?" I said, surprised. "Where in America? Was she writing to the military authorities?"

"Not a clue." Catchpole raised his hands in a helpless gesture. "The post came and went in a locked pouch, so we never saw the addresses."

I made a wry face. "If you never saw the addresses, then how did you know she was writing to America?"

"I asked her one day, and she said" — Catchpole's voice became sepulchral — " 'I'm sending a curse across the Atlantic, my lad, to damn those who betrayed me.' "

The old man's eyes gleamed menacingly in the lamplight, and I found myself shrinking away from him. He'd told us he believed in hatred, and at that moment I had no trouble believing him.

Beside me, Jamie stirred. "Why did your parents stay on, Catchpole? It couldn't have been pleasant for them to witness Miss DeClerke's decline."

Catchpole settled back in his chair. "My dad had no great love for Yanks. They twiddled their thumbs, he said, while England got pounded into a paste. They left the hard fighting to us, he said, then claimed they won the war."

"A lot of dead American soldiers would disagree with him," Wendy pointed out acerbically.

"I'm not saying Dad was right," said Catchpole, "but that's how he felt. Mother, she didn't care about such things, but she had a soft spot for Miss DeClerke. She'd raised her from a girl, you see, and couldn't leave her, not even when times got hard."

"I don't understand." I left my spoon in my empty bowl and gazed at Catchpole, perplexed. "Miss DeClerke was wealthy, wasn't she? She was an only child, the last of the line, so she must have inherited everything. Not that money can buy happiness, but . . ."

Wendy understood what I meant and asked bluntly: "How hard could times get for someone so rich?"

"She'd spent thousands of pounds on her wounded officers," Catchpole explained. "And with death duties and the income tax and the cost of running the abbey, her inheritance began to dry up. She sold off the London property and parcels of land around the valley, always to English buyers, but there came a time when she had to let the telephone go, then the electric. Twenty years ago she closed off most of the abbey and took to living in one set of rooms."

"Yet you stayed on," I said.

"Had to." Catchpole grunted. "After Dad and Mother died there was no one but me to look after Miss DeClerke. I had my cottage and I took on odd jobs in town to put food on the table. Miss DeClerke, though, she ended up in one room, living on tea and toast."

"Didn't she have anyone to advise her?" Wendy asked. "A family friend or a lawyer?"

"She wouldn't listen." Catchpole shook his head sadly. "National Trust came calling but she turned 'em down flat because they wouldn't agree to bar American tourists from the abbey. Then Miss Gibbs came along."

"An *English* actress," I murmured.

Catchpole nodded. "Took her three years to negotiate the sale. Miss DeClerke knew she was dying by then, but she still made Miss Gibbs promise to keep Yanks out of the abbey before she'd sell. I don't know if Miss Gibbs'll keep her part of the bargain, but, well, Miss DeClerke's been dead and gone these two years, so perhaps it doesn't matter so much anymore."

"It seems to matter to you," I said softly.

"I served Miss DeClerke for more than fifty years, madam. Old habits die hard." Catchpole laid his wrinkled hands flat on the table. "But Miss Gibbs is my mistress now, and I suppose I must learn to change with the times." He pushed himself to his feet. "I'll go up, now, and light the fires in your rooms, to take the chill off. I expect you'll be wanting to turn in early after such a bothersome day."

"Wait," said Jamie, rising. "I'll come up with you."

"So will I," said Wendy, and she went to the dresser to lift her backpack to her shoulders.

As I rose to join them, I noticed that my bowl was the only empty one on the table. Neither Wendy nor Jamie had eaten more than a spoonful of Catchpole's delectable dessert. Had the tragic tale of Miss DeClerke's demise robbed them of their appetites, I wondered, or were they still fretting about the murderous ghost?

I hesitated, then dragged my day pack toward me and resumed my seat. "If you don't mind coming back for me, Catchpole, I think I'll put in a call to my husband. I told him I'd phone at five and it's nearly that now."

"As you wish, madam." Catchpole raised a gnarled finger. "But don't go wandering off on your own. I wouldn't want you getting . . . *lost.*"

He loaded the final word with such intimations of doom that I half expected Jamie to drop his backpack and stand guard over me. Jamie must have had faith in my self-described toughness, though, because he responded to my confident smile with a friendly nod and left with the others.

I freely admit to suffering a brief nervous qualm as they shut the door behind them, leaving me alone in the vast kitchen with one flickering lamp and no matches, but it passed the moment I heard Bill's voice.

"Congratulations," he said cheerfully. "It's official. We're experiencing the worst snowstorm in the past hundred years."

"Yay," I said, with a marked lack of enthusiasm.

"Oh, come on, Lori," he coaxed. "You have to admit that it's pretty exciting. The whole country's shut down, from the Orkneys to the Scillies. Heathrow's closed to air traffic. Nothing's moving, not even the Royal Mail."

I sighed. "I guess the cottage is pretty low on the plowing priority list, then, huh?"

"We're waiting for plows to dig out the plows," Bill confirmed. "You're not running short on food, are you? I assume you and Wendy are pooling your resources."

"We haven't had to," I said. "There's plenty of food on hand. Your client keeps a full larder for her guests. Why didn't you tell me Tessa Gibbs bought Ladythorne Abbey?"

"It didn't seem important at the time," said Bill. "But I'm not surprised to hear about the bulging larder. Tessa likes to entertain."

"We won't starve," I agreed. "We may even put on weight. How are you and the boys holding up?"

"We ran low on milk this morning," Bill informed me, "but Emma and Derek skied over with a fresh supply."

"Why didn't they use the sleigh?" I asked.

"They can't get the horses out of the stables," Bill answered. "Will and Rob were so concerned about the horses that they made Emma promise to e-mail photographs of them as soon as she and Derek got home."

I hooted with laughter. "Little did Emma know what she'd be asked to do when she introduced the boys to riding."

"By the way," Bill continued, "she says you're right about the long distance trails. There aren't any near Ladythorne Abbey, but" — he repeated the word for emphasis — "*but* the valley's riddled with connecting trails. Emma thinks Wendy Walker must have been crossing from the Monarch Way to the Cotswolds Way or vice versa when the storm caught up with her. Aren't you pleased? You read the map correctly. Well done."

"Thanks," I said dryly, "but I've got a new puzzle for you. Remember Wendy's pry bar? The one she uses to split wood? Tell me, Mr. Smarty-pants: Why would she need to split wood if she's staying at hotels?"

"Has she been staying at hotels?" Bill asked.

"So she says," I replied.

"Maybe she plans to camp out later in the trip," Bill suggested.

I wrinkled my nose at the phone. Bill's

solution to the puzzle was so maddeningly obvious that I wanted to bang my head — or possibly his — against the table. It took a fair amount of self-discipline for me simply to change the subject. "Do you know anything about the DeClerke family? They owned the abbey before Tessa."

"I recognize the name from Tessa's contracts," said Bill, "but I never dealt with the family directly. Why?"

"Just curious," I replied. "There's a crazy old caretaker here who's been telling us stories about the DeClerkes. I wondered if any of them were true."

Bill paused before asking carefully, "How crazy is the caretaker, Lori?"

I looked up at the shotgun and asked myself if I really wanted a Special Forces arctic unit storming the abbey and taking Catchpole into custody.

"He's a little eccentric," I said lightly, "but he's been tremendously helpful. He cooked a scrumptious meal for us and he's upstairs now, lighting fires in our rooms."

"You may be stuck with this helpful crackpot for several days," Bill pointed out. "Are you sure you can cope with him?"

"He's a pussycat," I said, reasoning that even the fiercest lion had started out as a cub. "But I'd like to know more about the family he used to work for."

"The DeClerkes?" said Bill. "No problem. I'll make a few calls, see what I can find out. In the meantime, keep an eye on the caretaker."

"Will do," I promised, but as I glanced up from the phone, I saw that I'd already broken my promise.

Catchpole was standing in the doorway.

Six

I said good night to Bill and stood to face the caretaker.

"Hi," I said, wondering how long he'd been lurking in the doorway. "Fires lit?"

"They are," Catchpole said. "I've stoked the boiler as well, so you should have hot water by morning. If you're ready to go up . . ." He motioned for me to precede him into the corridor.

I donned my jacket, slung my day pack over my shoulders, picked up my oil lamp, and set it down again. With a boldness that surprised even me, I pushed a chair over to the white dresser, climbed onto it, and removed the shotgun from its high perch.

"Jamie asked me to bring the gun upstairs," I lied. I returned to the table to retrieve the lamp and headed for the corridor, carrying the shotgun in the crook of my arm. "I think he's a little nervous about firearms."

"Doesn't think I'm a pussycat, eh?" Catchpole growled.

I winced guiltily. "You heard that, did you? Sorry. I meant no disrespect, but you know how husbands are. They worry about the silliest things. I didn't want Bill to —"

"I'm grateful, madam." Catchpole stopped short and said earnestly, "I'm grateful to you for not telling him about the gun. Miss Gibbs would dismiss me if she knew I'd been such a nuisance to her attorney's wife, and it wouldn't be easy for me to find a new position at my age. I don't mind if your husband thinks I'm harmless. It's better than getting the sack."

If my hands hadn't been full, I would have mopped my brow. I'd expected Catchpole to bite my head off for branding him with such a condescending label, and I was greatly relieved that he'd taken it so well. At the same time, I felt a bit sorry for him. He was the kind of man who choked on swallowed pride, but he was clearly more afraid of losing his job than his dignity.

"Tessa won't sack you," I said encouragingly. "If she gets a taste of your risotto, Rhadu may be the one searching for a new position."

"It's kind of you to say so, madam," said Catchpole. "My mother taught me to cook. Had to turn my hand to every sort of work in Miss DeClerke's time, on account of there not being a full staff."

The old man's boots thudded heavily on the corridor's pine floorboards. The gloomy, low-ceilinged passageway was lined with doors that led to a warren of service rooms. Catchpole named some of them as we passed: scullery, boot room, lamp room, still room, servants' hall — the empty shells of what had once been a vital support system. Each door was shut, each room cloaked in silence. The corridor that had served as the main thoroughfare for a bustling army of servants was now a seldom-used back alley. I wouldn't have been surprised to see weeds sprouting between the floorboards.

Catchpole opened a door at the end of the corridor and we stepped into a high, square entrance hall that stopped me in my tracks. Nothing had prepared me for its splendor. The oak-paneled walls rose to a coffered ceiling dotted with brightly painted armorial medallions, and the oak staircase's gracefully turned banisters ended in a pair of exquisitely carved rosewood angels. One heavenly figure plucked a harp and the other blew an uplifted horn, as if heralding the arrival of Ladythorne's honored guests.

"Holy cow," I breathed.

My awestruck gasp seemed to please Catchpole. He held his lamp high and guided me to the center of the hall. His boots were silent on the encaustic tile floor, as if his very footsteps expressed his reverence for the great house beyond the service corridor.

I gaped like a guide-toting tourist, gazing wide-eyed at the finely crafted furnishings. A pair of tall Chinese vases filled with peacock feathers rested atop bloodred marble plant stands in the shadowy recess beneath the stairs, and a curlicued brass chandelier hung from the coved ceiling on a chunky chain. To my left, a gold-threaded tapestry hung above an altarlike console table that held a large, hand-beaten copper bowl and matching candlesticks. Directly ahead of me, a three-part stained glass window pierced the wall above a heavily carved door that would never have succumbed to Wendy's pry bar. Every object seemed flawless, every surface gleamed — there wasn't a cobweb in sight.

"I took the others up the back way," Catchpole said, "but I thought you might like to see what Miss Gibbs has done with the abbey. Wall panels were rotting away till she took charge. Replaced 'em all, from one end of the house to the other. Had to pull up most of the floors, too, and have 'em relaid."

"Amazing." I looked askance at the old man. "You don't have to do the dusting, do you?"

The pedestrian nature of my concern brought a faint twinkle to Catchpole's eye.

"Chars come in once a week," he informed me. "They were here yesterday — dusted, hoovered, aired the rooms. It's a good thing, too, because they won't be back till the plows get through."

I was oddly comforted by the notion of a troop of cleaning women rattling about the place and easing the old man's sense of isolation.

"It must be nice to have the company," I commented.

"I keep an eye on 'em," Catchpole growled. "Turn your back on those women for a minute and they'll steal the carpet from under your feet."

My rosy vision of chummy chats around the mop bucket popped like a soap bubble.

"Your room's on the first floor, madam," said Catchpole, and he led the way up the broad oak staircase.

"Tessa ought to get a medal," I declared as we ascended. "Or a knighthood or a . . .

a damehood. Anyone who saves an historic building should be rewarded in some way. She's preserved a national treasure."

"She's done Ladythorne proud," Catchpole agreed. "The furniture's still pretty rough in some of the rooms, but that's to be expected. Rome wasn't built in a day, my mother used to say."

I raised a hand to cover a yawn. "Sorry, Catchpole. I know it's only six o'clock, but I'm pooped."

"The others felt the same way," he told me. "I expect they're asleep already."

I hoped my fellow castaways were sound asleep because I didn't want anyone to overhear the little chat I intended to have as soon as I reached my room. While Bill made inquiries on his end, I planned to make use of my own, less orthodox, resources to find out more about the DeClerkes, and whereas a telephone conversation required no explanation, I'd have to plead insanity to explain a conversation with Aunt Dimity.

When we reached the top of the staircase, Catchpole turned right and proceeded down a corridor lined with linenfold oak paneling. There were no paintings on the walls, no side tables laden with glittering ornaments, and the floor runner, although luxuriously thick, was a plain, solid maroon. The effect was severe, almost claustrophobic, and served as a reminder of the abbey's original purpose. I was glad that Ladythorne's long-departed monks couldn't see me clomping through their sacred precincts in hiking boots, with a shotgun slung over my arm.

We'd gone no more than forty paces when Catchpole stopped at a door on our left.

"Here you are," he said. "Miss Walker's one door up from you. Mr. Macrae's across the hall. Bath and lavatory are next door to Miss Walker. You'll find clothes in the wardrobe, all spanking new. I'm sure something in there'll fit you. Feel free to use what you like. Miss Gibbs bought the lot for her guests."

"Where will you sleep tonight?" I asked.

"I'll go back to my cottage," Catchpole replied. "I've got budgies, you see, and their water'll need changing." He opened the door for me. "Good night, madam."

"Good night, Catchpole. Thanks for everything." I stepped across the threshold, turned, and put my head into the corridor, to watch until Catchpole and his flickering lamp began to descend the stairs. I couldn't help wondering if he was really going to wade through snowdrifts for the sake of his feathered friends, or if he'd invented the tale and planned instead to patrol the hallways till dawn, to make sure we kept to our rooms. Monks or no monks, I was suddenly quite pleased with myself for bringing the shotgun with me. The old man's mood swings were a bit too unpredictable for my peace of mind.

Once Catchpole had disappeared down the main staircase, I drew back from the threshold, closed the door, and turned to inspect my room. I'd half expected it to resemble a monk's cell, but it was as different from the severe corridor as it could be. Everything in it was light and airy, from the pretty floral wallpaper to the toile coverlet on the cream-painted bed. A plump armchair and a short-legged slipper chair, both upholstered in blue toile, sat on either side of a dainty tea table before the hearth. The skirted dressing table held a silver-backed hairbrush and hand mirror, and the marquetry writing table was neatly laid out with a silver pen and pencil set as well as a supply of ivory stationary embossed with a silhouette of Ladythorne's extraordinary roof line. A collection of Staffordshire figurines adorned the white-marble mantelpiece, and the fire burning in the grate filled the room with a rosy glow as well as welcome warmth.

The most striking thing about the room, however, was its silence. As I placed the oil lamp on the bedside table, slid the shotgun under the bed, and dropped my day pack on the slipper chair, I couldn't help noticing the extreme absence of sound. The refrigerator's hum, the furnace's intermittent rumble, the whoosh of water in pipes — all the familiar background noises I took for granted in my everyday life were missing. It was as if I'd been transported back to an earlier time, when silence was the rule, not the exception. If it hadn't been for the wind moaning at the windows and the fire snapping in the grate, I would have tapped my ears to make sure they were still working.

The windows overlooked the courtyard and the ramshackle outbuildings beyond. I parted the heavy drapes long enough to see great gouts of snow hurtling through the outer darkness, and closed them again, shivering. I was pleased to see that Catchpole had stocked the room with a full coal scuttle and a full box of wooden matches, ensuring that I wouldn't have to spend any part of the night without heat or light.

When I opened the wardrobe, I found

enough clothing to see me through a week's stay at the abbey. While I was sincerely grateful to my unwitting hostess for her farsightedness, I hoped with equal sincerity that I wouldn't need to take full advantage of it. I hung up my jacket and took off my hiking boots, but left the long white linen nightgown in the wardrobe. I wasn't ready to turn in just yet.

Reginald seemed to appreciate his release from captivity. His black button eyes glittered gratefully as I lifted him from the day pack and placed him on the tea table.

"Pretty quiet, huh, Reg?" I took the blue journal from the day pack, settled myself comfortably in the plump armchair, and held my stockinged feet out to the fire. "Emma thought solitude would be good for me, but right now I'd give twelve pots of gold to be reading bedtime stories to the boys." I gazed wistfully into the flames for a moment, then opened the journal. "Dimity? You'll never guess where we're spending the night."

Oh, Lori, you haven't gotten lost again, have you?

I smiled as the familiar loops and curls of royal-blue ink unfurled across the blank page, and thanked Bill silently for suggesting that Aunt Dimity accompany me on my grand day out.

Emma gave you a map, didn't she? I'm sure she told you to keep to the path.

"True," I acknowledged, "but she did *not* tell me about the blizzard."

Has there been a blizzard?

"The most blizzardy blizzard in the past one hundred years," I announced with a flourish. "If they were giving prizes for blizzards, this one would win Best in Show. It's closed down the whole country, so you can hardly blame me for losing my way in it. We're snowbound, Dimity. We're snowbound in Ladythorne Abbey."

Ladythorne Abbey? You astound me. Is it still standing? I thought it had fallen to bits years ago.

"Nope," I said. "It's in fine shape. You should see the entrance hall. It's stunning. I'll tell you, those monks knew a thing or two about interior decorating."

What monks?

"The monks who built the abbey."

Ladythorne wasn't built by monks, my dear. It isn't a real abbey. It never was. It's a Gothic-revival Victorian imitation.

"No monks, then?" I said, mildly disappointed.

Not one, unless someone was playing at fancy-dress. Gothic architecture was enor-

mously popular in the nineteenth century. Those who could afford to built faux castles and priories and abbeys — anything that smacked of the romantically medieval.

"When was Ladythorne built?" I hunkered down in the chair, fascinated.

The abbey was built in 1874 by a man who'd made his fortune supplying unmentionables to Her Majesty's armed forces. He started life as Grundy Clerk, but changed the family surname to DeClerke when he took up residence in the abbey. I imagine he wanted his name to reflect his rise in the world.

"In other words, he was a self-made Victorian snob," I said.

To the contrary: by all accounts, he was a good and decent man. He gave generously to charities, ran his business ethically, looked after his older workers, and remained married to the same woman for fifty-seven years. Grundy and Rose DeClerke raised four sons, but three of them, alas, were killed in the Great War. Only one survived, young Neville DeClerke. Neville inherited everything upon Grundy's death, including, I'm happy to say, his father's integrity.

"He was an ethical businessman," I commented.

He was, but I'm speaking of integrity on a more personal level. Neville's wife died of the

Spanish influenza only a month after giving birth to their only child, a daughter. Neville must have longed for a son and heir, but he never remarried. He remained faithful to his first love until his own tragic death in the early days of the Blitz.

"What was his daughter's name?" I asked.

Lucasta. Lucasta Eleanora DeClerke. She's a somewhat unusual woman. Though it grieves me to say it, I wouldn't have expected her to allow you to take shelter in the abbey, however terrible the blizzard.

"She didn't." I paused before adding gently, "What I mean is, I'm sorry, Dimity, but Lucasta DeClerke died two years ago."

Oh, dear. The firelight quivered as a faint breeze wafted through the room, the ghost of a sigh. *Poor Lucasta. The DeClerke name died with her, I'm afraid. Such a brief flowering. Withered away in only three generations . . .*

I waited in respectful silence while Dimity absorbed the sad news, then looked sharply toward the corridor. Had a floorboard creaked, just outside my room? A tiny finger of fear trailed down my spine. If a floorboard had creaked, it meant that someone had stepped off of the luxuriant runner to stand close to my door.

"Wait," I said, under my breath. "I think someone may be listening."

We're not alone? Who else

I closed the journal and set it next to Reginald on the tea table, crept toward the door, and pressed my ear to the white-painted wood. The creaking floorboard had gone silent. Whoever had trodden on it had evidently moved on.

"Catchpole," I whispered, and resentment flared.

In my head, my husband's voice quietly enumerated the reasons why I should shove the slipper chair under the door-knob, climb into bed, and cower beneath the covers, but his sage advice was drowned out by clamoring indignation. My blood boiled as I pictured Catchpole with his eye to the keyhole, hoping to catch a glimpse of me slipping into the linen night-gown. If he thought his role as caretaker gave him the right to play Peeping Tom, he was in for the shock of his life.

I flung the door wide, marched into the hall, and turned toward the staircase just in time to see a light flicker like a will-o-the-wisp in the inky blackness far down the corridor, then vanish.

I tapped my foot, incensed by his effron-tery, then ran to fetch the small flashlight

Emma had tucked into my pack for emergencies, muttering grimly, "Okay, you old coot, let's see how *you* like being spied on."

Seven

I shielded the flashlight's narrow beam with my hand and slipped into the corridor, closing the door behind me. My bootless feet didn't make a sound as I trotted past the staircase to the point at which I thought the will-o-the-wisp had vanished, and a surge of triumph coursed through me when I saw a thin strip of light beneath a door on my left.

"Aha!" I exclaimed, and burst into the room like the heroine in a melodrama, ready to point an accusing finger at the evildoer.

Jamie Macrae looked up from his seat by the fire. He was wearing the same cobalt-blue sweater and faded jeans he'd worn upon his arrival at Ladythorne Abbey, and his oil lamp was burning steadily on a table at his elbow.

"Hullo," he said, in mild surprise. "I thought you'd gone to bed."

"Uh . . ." I lowered my accusing finger. "No."

"I couldn't sleep, either — all the excitement, I suppose, and the early hour — so I went in search of the library." He set aside the book he'd been reading and let his gaze travel around the room. "It's lovely, isn't it? It'll be a pity when the electricity's restored. Some rooms are meant to be seen by firelight."

Some men, too, were meant to be seen by firelight. The shifting shadows gave a liquid shimmer to Jamie's dark eyes. The shivering flames lit ruddy sparks in his long hair and tinted his fair skin with warm peach tones. It took some effort to tear my gaze away from him and notice the room, but when I did, I gave a soft gasp of pleasure.

Ladythorne's library was every bit as splendid as its entrance hall. Elegant glass-enclosed mahogany bookcases lined the walls, but they seemed dull and ordinary compared to the breathtaking mosaic that filled the space above them to the ceiling. The glorious mosaic depicted Chaucer's pilgrims on their journey to Canterbury — the Knight in his stained tunic, the fashionable young Squire with his freshly curled locks, the hearty Monk, the dainty Nun, the lusty Wife of Bath, and the rest, each character kissed and brought to vivid life by the flickering flames.

The firelight glinted from each brightly colored tile, sent fugitive gleams along the lustrous mahogany, and enriched the jewel tones of the Turkey carpet covering the parquet floor. The mosaic's brilliance added warmth to the more subtle colors of the calf-bound books and set off the simplicity of the stone fireplace. The fireplace's sole decoration was a quotation carved deeply into the mantel shelf in Celtic script.

" 'A good book is the best of friends,' " Jamie read aloud, following my gaze, " 'the same today and forever.' A splendid sentiment credited to one M. F. Tupper, but who M. F. Tupper is, I've no idea."

"Martin Farquhar Tupper," I said, without thinking. "A minor Victorian writer. Big on proverbs."

Jamie's eyes widened.

"I used to work with old books," I explained, blushing. "My head is packed solid with useless information."

"Why is it that the only information worth knowing is deemed useless? I'd much rather learn about dear old Martin Farquhar than the workings of a computer chip." Jamie held out his hand to the leather armchair that faced his across the hearth. "Won't you join me?"

I closed the hall door, stowed my flashlight in the pocket of my jeans, and sat in the armchair, wondering if Jamie was going to ask why I'd burst in on him like an avenging angel or politely pretend that he hadn't noticed.

"I stopped by your room a few minutes ago," he said. "I was looking for company, but I heard you on the phone with your husband and didn't want to intrude."

"It was you?" My faint blush deepened to crimson. "I thought you were Catchpole playing Peeping Tom. That's why I came charging in here. I was going to wring his neck."

Jamie clucked his tongue. "I wouldn't advise it. I'm told neck-wringing isn't conducive to a good night's sleep."

I smiled sheepishly, then cocked my head to one side. "I hope you don't mind my saying so, Jamie, but your accent confuses me. Or maybe it's your speech pattern. For an American, you sound very . . . English."

"My mother was English." Jamie stretched his legs out toward the fire, folded his hands across his dark-blue sweater, and leaned back in his chair. "My parents met in England during the war, wrote to each other afterward, fell in love, and were married. She came to America to live, of course — the classic G.I. bride — but we kept in close touch with her family in England and visited often. I studied at Oxford as well, so I suppose I can't help being a mongrel."

"I'm not complaining," I said, and I wasn't. Jamie's voice was beautifully deep and resonant. I wanted to ask him to read aloud from his book, just for the pleasure of hearing him speak, but chose to achieve the same goal more gracefully by simply keeping the conversation going for as long as possible.

"Both of my parents served during the war," I said. "My mother was on Eisenhower's staff in London and my dad landed at Omaha Beach on D-day."

"You must be proud of both of them," said Jamie. "Did they want you to serve in the military?"

"I don't think anyone's ever pictured *me* in uniform," I said, laughing. "Did your dad expect you to join up?"

"No," said Jamie. "In fact, he was very much against it."

"I'm glad," I said, without thinking.

"Are you?" Jamie gave me a questioning look. "Why?"

"Because . . ." I hadn't known him long enough to confess that the mere thought of those soft, dark curls falling victim to a buzz cut made me want to gnash my teeth and howl, so I said airily, "Because it's a dangerous profession."

"True," Jamie agreed. "It wouldn't have suited me, in any case. I prefer woodland walks to obstacle courses, and I'm no good at following orders. I'd've made a rotten soldier."

"I'm not so sure about that," I said. "You impressed the heck out of me when Catchpole was waving his gun around. You were so calm, and you disarmed him so easily."

"Did I seem calm?" Jamie stroked his beard reflectively. "I suppose I was. Father taught me basic self-defense, so I wasn't quite as rattled by Catchpole's antics as you appeared to be."

"I wasn't rattled," I stated flatly. "I was scared spitless. That's why I brought the shotgun up to my room. It's under my bed."

"What a good idea." Jamie nodded. "I should have thought of it."

"It comes from being a mother," I said. "I never leave dangerous toys where little boys can get at them."

Jamie laughed. "How many children do you have?"

"Two," I said. "Twin four-year-olds named Will and Rob, and don't get me started on them or you'll soon be pleading with me to wring your neck."

We talked about the boys nonetheless. Jamie, evidently a glutton for punishment, demanded to hear more, and I acquiesced, curling my legs beneath me and serving up my best anecdotes for his entertainment. Even as I spoke, I savored the irony — my paranoia about Catchpole had resulted in a thoroughly enjoyable encounter. Jamie's companionable presence brought to mind my first trip to England, when I'd stayed up all night in youth hostels, holding intimate discussions with perfect strangers whose paths would never again cross mine. There was something about lousy weather and damp socks that instantly transformed the most casual of acquaintances into the closest of friends.

"It's a pity you can't be home this evening," Jamie observed, when I'd finally lapsed into silence. "Your husband and sons must miss you."

"Believe me, it's mutual," I said. "My husband travels a lot because of his job, so having him at home is a special treat. I hate missing it. Are you married?"

"No." He shrugged. "I came close to it a

few years ago, but my father fell ill and I spent so much time looking after him that I had no time left to look after my fiancée. She was understandably annoyed, and the thing rather fell through."

Jamie's wistful expression brought to mind a few choice comments about worthless, heartless fiancées, but I said only, "Is your father all right?"

"He died two months ago. Shortly before Christmas." Jamie turned his head to gaze fixedly into the fire. "It was a merciful release. Alzheimer's."

The last word contained such a world of weariness that a shadow seemed to dim the bright mosaic. Jamie's eyes darkened, too, despite the firelight, as if he'd been to a place light couldn't reach and hadn't yet found a way out.

"I'm sorry," I said quietly. "It must have been hard to lose him like that."

"I wouldn't wish it on my worst enemy." Jamie tossed his hair back from his face and went on briskly, "I came over to England to take a long walk and clear my head. I didn't expect to end up at the abbey, but it makes a pleasant change from the VA hospital."

"I'm sure it does. Did your father reminisce about the war? He must have had a lot of stories to tell." I checked myself, then added hastily, "If you'd rather not talk about him, Jamie, just say the word and I'll go back to the perils of potty-training."

Jamie smiled. "I don't mind talking about my father. Sometimes it helps to talk about him. No, he never spoke of the war. I think he wanted to shield me from the horrors he'd witnessed. My mother told me about it, though, and she knew a great deal. As Catchpole pointed out earlier, England had been fighting desperately for three years before the Yanks made their first appearance."

I nodded wisely. "That must be why you know so much about Dunkirk and the Blitz."

"I've done a fair amount of reading on the subject," said Jamie. "I'm interested in history."

"Me, too," I said, pleased to discover that we had something else in common. "Is your mother still alive?"

"Very much so," said Jamie. "She's eighty-seven, but she's in good health and her mind's as sharp as a razor. She encouraged me to take this trip. She said I needed to get the stench of nursing homes out of my nostrils." He looked up at the mosaic.

"She'd love it here. She's always loved Chaucer."

I craned my neck to look at the book Jamie had set aside when I'd burst in on him. "Is that a photo album?"

"It is." Jamie glanced at the large volume, but made no move to pick it up. "I found it on one of the shelves. It helped pass the time until you arrived."

"It looks old," I said.

"It belonged to the DeClerkes," he told me. "I'm not sure what Tessa Gibbs is doing with it."

"My husband said that Tessa bought the house and its contents," I informed him. "The books in the library must count as contents." I held out my hand. "May I see it? I love looking at old pictures. They help me feel connected to the past."

"Why don't we look at it together?" Jamie motioned for me to join him as he moved from his chair to the floor.

We sat side by side on the Turkey carpet, turning the pages of the old morocco-bound album and marveling at the images it contained. It was a DeClerke family memento, a collection of full-length portrait photographs taken at a fancy-dress ball held at the abbey in 1897 to celebrate Queen Victoria's Diamond Jubilee.

All of the guests were fabulously attired, but I was particularly captivated by a photograph of the hosts: Grundy DeClerke and his wife, Rose. The handwritten caption below the photograph described them as the personifications of Night and Day, but their costumes might have been designed solely to display the wealth Grundy had amassed selling unmentionables to Her Majesty's armed forces. Grundy's short cape, pierced doublet, and flat cap were made of lavishly embroidered and bejeweled black velvet — even his black stockings were patterned with pearls.

Rose, however, would have outshone the sun. A froth of ostrich feathers spouted from her glittering tiara, jewel-encrusted bracelets encircled her sturdy wrists, her bodice was bracketed by a pair of sunburst brooches, her dimpled fingers were laden with rings, and teardrop diamonds as big as my thumbnail hung from her earlobes. She wore a trailing, ermine-edged white velvet cape over a wasp-waisted white gown. The gown's plunging neckline revealed almost all there was to see of her ample bosom, but her personal attractions were overshadowed by the stunning necklace that spilled, like a waterfall of diamonds, from the diamond-studded choker around her neck.

The necklace, like the tiara, had been crafted to resemble a fan of peacock feathers, and a pair of real peacocks had been posed at the couple's feet, as if to underscore the theme. The birds stood erect, their long tails draped artistically across the marble floor, their small, pointed beaks cocked smugly toward the camera, blithely unaware that they were playing second fiddle to the breathtaking diamonds adorning Rose DeClerke.

"I dressed up as a cat last Halloween," I said with a sigh. "How times have changed."

"Conspicuous consumption isn't what it used to be," Jamie agreed, and turned the page. "Look. Their sons."

I gazed soberly at four boys of varying ages who appeared together in one sepia-toned photograph, dressed as medieval pages. Three of them, I knew, would soon be lying dead in the mud of Flanders. The fourth would lose his life years later in the Blitz, leaving behind a daughter who would one day lose her mind.

"I wonder what happened to Lucasta," I murmured, forgetting for a moment that I'd learned Miss DeClerke's first name from a highly classified source.

"Lucasta?" Jamie closed the album. "Who's Lucasta?"

"Miss DeClerke," I replied, and covered my blunder by saying that Catchpole had mentioned his former employer's Christian name to me on the way up to my room. "Why did she go crazy?" I took my lower lip between my teeth and glanced anxiously at Jamie. "You don't suppose she was . . . raped . . . do you?"

"No, I do not," he said firmly. "The military authorities wouldn't be able to hush up something like that. Lucasta wasn't a shop girl, after all. She was an extremely wealthy heiress who was running a convalescent home staffed by army personnel. If she'd been assaulted by an American, no one could have swept it under the carpet."

"I hope you're right," I said.

Jamie's arm brushed mine as he moved forward to add coal to the fire and I felt an all-too-familiar tingle of physical attraction. Only a week-old corpse, I reasoned, could fail to be attracted to someone as appealing as Jamie Macrae in such an absurdly romantic setting, but I put the brakes on my natural impulses and moved away from him to sit with my back against the seat of my chair. I wondered idly if the young Lucasta and her noble husband-to-be had spent time together in this library, gazing up at the brilliant mosaic and sharing dreams for the future.

"Maybe Lucasta fell in love with one of her patients," I mused aloud, "and maybe he rejected her. It would have been a pretty devastating blow, coming so soon after losing her fiancé at Dunkirk."

"Unrequited love can be devastating," Jamie said, so sadly that I wished I hadn't spoken.

I'd forgotten about his worthless fiancée. I reached out to lay a comforting hand on his shoulder and nearly clipped him in the jaw as a loud *bang!* reverberated through the corridor.

"Was that a gunshot?" I said. "You don't suppose Catchpole —" I broke off, heart racing, and looked fearfully toward the hall. "Where's Wendy?"

"I'll find out." Jamie's dark eyes flashed with anger as he sprang nimbly to his feet. "You stay here and bar the door. I'm going to put an end to Catchpole's antics once and for all."

Eight

Jamie might have been lousy at following orders, but he was awfully good at giving them. Even though I preferred to be in the front lines, flailing, when the trump of battle sounded, on this occasion I followed his instructions to the letter. I remained in the library, shoved a heavy chair against the door, armed myself with the poker from the fireplace, and waited in breathless anticipation for whatever might happen next. What happened next almost frightened me out of my socks.

Jamie had been gone for scarcely five minutes when I heard a footstep in the corridor. I raised the poker high and watched in horrid fascination as the doorknob slowly turned, first one way, then the other. When the door bumped hard against the chair, I nearly shrieked.

"Jamie?" a voice whispered.

"Wendy?" I whispered back.

"Lori?" said Wendy.

"Oh, thank God . . ." My poker arm

drooped like a wilting tulip and I heaved a tremulous sigh of relief. "Yes, it's Lori."

"What are you doing here?" Wendy asked. "Where's Jamie?"

"Jamie and I were talking," I answered. "He's gone to rescue you and to beat the tar out of Catchpole."

"Rescue me? Catchpole?" A note of exasperation entered Wendy's voice. "Let me in, will you? I feel ridiculous, talking through a door."

"Sorry." I pulled the chair aside, but pushed it back as soon as Wendy was safely in the room.

Her long gray hair was still wound in an elaborate knot at the nape of her neck and she was wearing the same clothes she'd worn earlier, with the curious addition of what appeared to be a miner's lamp strapped to her head. I restrained the urge to ask about the lamp because I didn't want to be told that it was, like the pry bar, just another standard piece of gear carried by *truly intelligent* backpackers, i.e., not me. Besides, Wendy was eyeing me as if I'd lost my marbles.

"Why are you barricading us in the library?" she asked, in the appeasing tone of voice usually reserved for the dangerously dotty.

"Catchpole's on the rampage," I told her. "Didn't you hear the gunshot?"

Wendy rolled her eyes to the heavens, then reached up to switch off her miner's lamp. "It wasn't a gunshot. It was a blanket chest."

"A what?" I said, blinking stupidly.

"A blanket chest." Wendy moved the chair away from the door and strode over to hold her hands out to the fire. "My bedroom was chilly, so I went looking for extra blankets. I spotted a big wooden chest at the end of the corridor and took a look inside. The lid slipped and came crashing down. That's all." She looked at me over her shoulder. "You can put the poker away. I don't think you'll be needing it — unless you're afraid of blanket chests."

I greeted her witticism with a thin smile and returned the poker to its stand by the fireplace. Wendy seemed to be going out of her way to make me feel like the original hysterical woman.

"Call me a sissy," I said, "but when I hear something that sounds like a gunshot, I get a little nervous. I have a healthy respect for firearms."

"So do I," Wendy retorted. "But I'm not afraid of them."

I folded my arms and said with heavy

irony, "I imagine you were cool as a cucumber when Catchpole was waving his shotgun around."

"As a matter of fact, I was." Wendy turned her back to the fire. "He couldn't've shot us even if the gun *had* been loaded. The safety catch was on."

I let my arms fall to my sides in defeat. Wendy sent satellites into orbit, knitted her own sweaters, and designed her own backpacks. She'd figured out how to work a complicated Victorian range in less time than it had taken me to figure out how to operate my microwave. Were there no limits to her competence?

"You know about guns, too?" I said wanly.

"My father was a marksman," she replied with annoying nonchalance. "We always had guns around the house. He taught me how to shoot."

I looked at her in alarm. "You're not carrying a gun in your backpack, are you?"

"In England? Not likely." Wendy bent to lift the morocco-bound photo album from the floor. She leafed through a few pages, then set it on the table beside Jamie's chair, as if it held no interest for her. "What were you and Jamie talking about? Life, the universe, and everything?"

I bridled at the hint of mockery in her tone, but replied civilly, "More or less. We ended up talking about Miss DeClerke, though — trying to figure out what happened to her."

Wendy stepped away from the fire and sat in Jamie's chair, facing me. "Did you come up with any answers?"

"Not really." I turned toward the fire, disconcerted by Wendy's headgear. It was as if I were being interrogated by a Cyclops. "My best guess is that she fell in love with one of the American officers during his stay here. He rejected her and she couldn't take it, not after losing her fiancé and her father. So she went a little nuts and spent the rest of her life writing letters to the guy, reproaching him or cajoling him or" — I sank into my chair — "or maybe they were love letters. Who knows?"

"How romantic," Wendy murmured sardonically. She ruminated in silence for a moment, then shook her head and said, "What a waste. What a stupid, tragic waste. She had so much" — Wendy swept a hand through the air to indicate Ladythorne in general — "but she wasn't satisfied. She could have made something of her life, something important and valuable, but she wasted it on a futile obsession. I don't get it."

"I do." I resented Wendy's cold assessment of Lucasta's plight and felt driven to defend the dead woman. "It's not uncommon for a war hero to crack up when the war ends."

"Don't tell me you think of Miss DeClerke as a war hero," Wendy said, incredulous.

"Why not?" I said heatedly. "She nursed a lot of wounded men back to health. She turned her home into a sanctuary for them. She gave them everything she had for the duration of the war and then, *bang*, it was over, they were gone, and everything came crashing in on her, all her losses, all her pain. She realized at gut level, maybe for the first time, that the men she'd lost were *never coming back*." I felt my throat constrict in a spasm of sympathy. "It'd be enough to drive anyone over the edge."

"If you say so," Wendy said, in a subdued murmur.

We sat in silence. It wasn't the companionable silence I'd shared with Jamie, but an awkward, prickly silence. I was struggling to regain my composure, and Wendy, I suspected, was holding her tongue for fear that I'd snap at her if she made anymore insensitive comments about Lucasta DeClerke.

"I'm sorry," I said after a time. "I shouldn't have spoken so . . . forcefully. The thing is, my father fought in the war. If he'd been wounded, I would have gone down on my knees to thank anyone who helped him. So I find it hard to be detached about Miss DeClerke."

"I cultivate detachment," Wendy said airily. "My job demands it. Sloppy sentimentality won't steady a wobbly satellite; clear thinking often will. If you choose to romanticize Miss DeClerke, that's your business, but don't ask me to join in."

I returned her condescending gaze with a defiant one of my own. Wendy Walker might understand inanimate objects, but she had a lot to learn about the human heart. Her callous dismissal of Lucasta's tragic life appalled me. If I hadn't wanted to say good night to Jamie, I would have gladly left Wendy to her own devices and gone to my room. But I stayed on, for Jamie's sake, and seethed in resentful silence as she switched on her headlamp and went to the door to look for him.

"No sign of him," she reported, and resumed her seat.

"What made you think he'd be here in

the library?" I asked. "Catchpole told me you'd both gone to bed."

"We had, but . . ." Wendy bent to fiddle with her boot lace. "But when I went to look for blankets, I saw the light down here and thought one of you had gone exploring. You don't strike me as a very brave little toaster, so I assumed I'd find Jamie in here. That's why I said his name first." She sat up. "I wonder where he is?"

"Searching for Catchpole," I said. "He was ready to lock the old man in the coal hole."

"He can't do that," Wendy protested. "Not before Catchpole makes breakfast for us, anyway."

I smiled dutifully, but I couldn't relax. Wendy's abrasive comments — I considered myself an extremely brave little toaster — had reawakened my earlier suspicions. Her use of the pry bar still niggled at me, and the queer miner's headlamp seemed like the sort of tool a burglar would use to keep his hands free while stuffing the family silver into his swag bag — or his backpack. Her story about searching for extra blankets seemed fishy, too. Why would she need extra blankets, I asked myself, when she had a perfectly good sleeping bag strapped to her pack frame?

"Did you find the blankets you were looking for?" I inquired, wondering if she'd used the pry bar to break into the chest.

"No," Wendy replied. "The chest was empty. That's why the lid made such a loud noise when it fell." She swung sideways and draped her legs over the arm of Jamie's chair. "I guess I'll have to use my sleeping bag tonight. I was hoping to find something more luxurious, like an antique quilt or a big, puffy duvet."

Curses, I thought, foiled again. Every time I came up with a good reason to regard Wendy with suspicion, a better reason came along to take her at face value.

Aloud, I said, "Jamie found the album you were looking at. Fascinating, isn't it?"

"Not to me." Wendy looked askance at the morocco-bound album. "Old photographs give me the creeps. The people in them are so stiff and . . . dead-looking. I feel as if I'm touring a morgue."

"I have to admit that I never thought of it that way," I said diplomatically, and wrote Wendy off as a Philistine to whom I had nothing more to say.

From a conversational point of view, it

was fortunate that Jamie chose that moment to return.

"So this is where you've been," he said as his gaze fell upon Wendy. "I've been looking for you everywhere. Catchpole —"

"— is probably snoring in his own bed by now," Wendy interrupted, and calmly recounted her encounter with the blanket chest for Jamie's benefit.

He wasn't nearly as surprised by her explanation as I had been.

"I didn't think it was a gunshot," he said. "It sounded more like a door slamming. I thought Catchpole might have been chasing you through the house."

"I haven't seen Catchpole since he took us to our rooms." Wendy got to her feet. "Which is where I'm going now. I don't know about you two, but I'm ready to hit the sack."

"Try to get there quietly, will you?" Jamie requested.

"I'll do my best. See you in the morning." Wendy's headlamp flared as she entered the murky corridor, leaving Jamie and me to make up our own minds about whether or not to turn in.

I waited a moment, then crossed to look into the corridor, to make sure Wendy wasn't listening at the keyhole. Satisfied by the sight of her headlamp floating toward the bedrooms, I closed the door and favored Jamie with a speculative gaze.

"Do you trust Wendy?" I asked.

"In what way?" he said.

"I don't know. . . ." I clasped my hands behind my back and paced deliberately between the door and the hearth. "I have a funny feeling that she's not telling us the truth."

Jamie followed me. "About what?"

"About why she came here," I said abruptly. "About why she carries a pry bar and straps a weird lamp-thingy to her head instead of using a flashlight like a normal person. About why she's poking around in blanket chests when she has a sleeping bag." I rubbed my chin thoughtfully. "Now that I think of it, she didn't give me a straight answer about the gun, either."

"Gun?" Jamie said. "What gun?"

"I asked her if she had a gun in her backpack and she said 'Not likely.' That's not a straight answer, is it?" I shook my head. "And I don't believe her room is cold. Mine's as warm as toast."

"It won't be if you neglect the fire much longer." Jamie put his arm around me and gave me a good-natured shake. "Let's slow down for a moment, Lori. Let's take a deep breath, shall we? Is it possible, do you think, that our unusual situation may be coloring your judgment? Don't you think you may be reading too much into things you wouldn't otherwise notice? I'm not teasing you — I feel it myself." He loosed his hold and let his gaze traverse the room. "The silence, the shadows, the isolation — they weave a powerful spell. It's bound to conjure some strange imaginings. I'm certain you'll think of Wendy differently in the clear light of day."

I remained stubbornly silent for a moment, then gave a reluctant nod. "You may be right about Wendy. I know you're right about the fire in my room; I should get back before it dies down. Unlike some people I could mention, I don't have a sleeping bag to rely on."

"I'll come with you." Jamie banked the fire, picked up his oil lamp, and escorted me back up the corridor. When we reached my room, he paused and bent his head close to mine.

"If you feel a chill coming on in the night," he said softly, "feel free to knock on my door." I was about to utter a courteous, if not entirely heartfelt, thanks-but-no-thanks, when Jamie deflated my latest imagining by adding, "There must be a dozen extra blankets on top of my wardrobe. You're welcome to them all."

"I'm sure I'll be fine," I said, hoping the floor would swallow me whole before Jamie took note of my blushes. "Sleep well."

"You, too." He smiled warmly and went to his room.

I scuttled into my own room, closed the door, and leaned against it, cringing with embarrassment. I'd come within a hairsbreadth of turning down an invitation that Jamie had clearly had no intention of making. How could I have imagined, even for a moment, that he would consider making a pass at me? Who did I think I was? Miss Irresistible?

Jamie Macrae wasn't a hormone-addled teenager. He was a grown man, and a gentleman, to boot. Apart from that, he was still recovering from the agonizing ordeal of watching his father succumb to the ravages of Alzheimer's disease. It was extremely doubtful that he'd be in the mood for a spot of hanky-panky with anyone, let alone a happily married mother of twins, who most certainly would have rejected the offer, had he made it in the first place, which he hadn't.

"Get a grip," I muttered, and carefully

avoided Reginald's eyes.

I couldn't avoid looking at the blue journal, however. It seemed to glow with impatience and I realized, with a wince, that nearly three hours had passed since I'd heard Jamie outside my bedroom door. I tossed coal onto the dwindling fire, shifted the oil lamp from the bedside table to the tea table, and threw myself into the plump armchair. I took a brief moment to catch my breath, then opened the journal very gently, hoping Dimity wouldn't be too put out with me for abandoning her at such a suspenseful moment.

"Dimity?" I said tentatively. "I'm sorry for taking so long to get back to you. It turned out to be a false alarm. That is, someone *was* at my door, but it wasn't who I thought it was, it was someone else."

I watched in dismay as the lines of royal-blue ink appeared on the blank page. Dimity's flowing copperplate had turned ominously crisp and formal — a sure sign that she was not the happiest of campers.

Nine

Who, precisely, is snowbound with us, Lori? Dimity's clipped handwriting brought to mind a schoolmarm's snappish voice. *A band of vagabonds? A Boy Scout troop? The wind section of the London Philharmonic?*

"I'm sorry," I repeated. "What happened was, Jamie and I got to talking and we lost track of —"

Jamie, is it? Now I understand. Don't tell me, let me guess. Tall? Dark? Handsome? Oh, and let's not forget charming. They're always charming, aren't they?

I knew that Dimity's fit of pique had been brought on by prolonged worry, and that her chosen theme was based on the few close encounters of the whoops!-I-forgot-I'm-married kind I'd had with a handful of men in the past. I'd never broken my vows to Bill, but Dimity was painfully aware of the number of times I'd bent them, so I couldn't resent her observations or accuse her of hurling groundless innuendoes.

"Jamie Macrae is all of those things," I said evenly, "but he's also in his room and I'm in mine and never the twain shall meet, so to speak, except on the most platonic, blanket-borrowing level. Okay? Besides, he's not the only one here. There's an American backpacker named Wendy Walker and a crotchety old caretaker who looks after the place." I paused briefly before adding, sotto voce, "The philharmonic's stuck in London."

When Dimity's handwriting resumed, it scrolled across the page in its usual graceful manner, and I knew that one storm, at least, had blown over.

I apologize for my intemperate outburst, my dear, but I've been terribly concerned about you. You must tell me what's going on. Why did you tear out of here in such a lather? Where have you been? Why were you gone for such a long time?

I sent up a silent prayer of thanks for Dimity's forgiving nature, settled Reginald in the crook of my left arm, and said, "I thought the old caretaker was spying on me through the keyhole, so I lost my temper and went after him — to give him a piece of my mind and maybe a smack in the chops. But it wasn't him, after all. It was Jamie."

I see. There was a brief pause. *Jamie was spying on you through the keyhole?*

"No!" I exclaimed, and hurriedly explained what Jamie had been doing. "He heard me talking to you and thought I was talking to Bill. He didn't want to interrupt my tête-à-tête with my husband, so he went to the library by himself. Jamie's thoughtful and courteous, Dimity, which is more than I can say for Wendy, the other backpacker. She's a real pain in the —" A jaw-stretching yawn silenced my own intemperate outburst.

Needless to say, I'm champing at the bit to hear more about Wendy, but it sounds to me as though you should be in bed, Lori. You must be extremely tired after your difficult day.

"Ridiculous, but true." I glanced blearily at my watch. "It's not even nine o'clock yet, but it feels like midnight. I guess the blizzard knocked the stuffing out of me."

I'm glad it did nothing worse. Pleasant dreams, dear girl.

"Thanks, Dimity." I waited until the lines of royal-blue ink had faded from the page, then closed the journal and got ready for bed. As I crawled beneath the covers, I wondered if I'd have trouble sleeping in a place devoid of normal, everynight noises.

I didn't.

* * *

I rolled over sleepily to drape an arm over Bill and noticed two things at once: Bill wasn't there, and our bedroom was a lot colder than usual. Shivering, I slid my arm back under the covers, nestled my head more deeply into the soft, welcoming pillow, and made a mental note to have Mr. Barlow check the cottage's central heating first thing in the morning. I was on the verge of dozing off when the sound of muted voices reached my ears.

I opened my eyes and peered, perplexed, at the toile coverlet, then sat up abruptly as reality asserted itself. I wasn't at home, snug in bed with my husband. I was in a strange bed in a strange bedroom in a strange place called Ladythorne Abbey. And I seemed to be wearing someone else's nightgown.

As my memory of the previous day's events slowly clicked into place, I realized that the muted voices coming from the corridor belonged to my two housemates. Jamie Macrae and Wendy Walker were holding a quiet conversation outside my door, but as I bent my ear to listen, they moved beyond my range of hearing, leaving only one audible word floating behind them.

"Breakfast," I echoed, and my stomach promptly reminded me that my last meal had, in its opinion, taken place far too long ago. I lifted my watch from the bedside table and saw that it was nearly seven o'clock.

"Ten hours of sleep is enough for anyone, right Reg?" I twiddled my pink bunny's ears and hopped out of bed, confident that my resourceful companions would have a pot of tea brewing by the time I joined them.

The fire had burned low in the night, so I heaped it with coals before pulling on a clean pair of woolen socks and a long woolen dressing gown from the wardrobe. I waited until the flames were leaping, then padded up the hall to the bathroom.

I'd been too tired to take note of the bathroom's decor the night before, so it came as a delightful surprise to see the pretty enameled tiles covering the walls, the tub with its mahogany surround, and the classic pedestal sink. The toilet and bidet were housed in a separate room next door, a sensible arrangement for those who enjoyed long baths free from interruption.

I found fresh towels in a wall cupboard and a tempting array of toiletries — clearly chosen with a woman's desires in mind —

in a hand-painted, three-drawer dresser beside the sink. I gazed longingly at the exotic bath salts, luxury shampoos, and fragrant lotions, but decided against making full use of them. Although Catchpole's industrious boiler-stoking had provided ample hot water, I was put off by the thought of rising from a steamy bath into air crisp enough to freshen lettuce.

After a quick wash-and-brush-up I returned to the bedroom to dress. I put on my own jeans, then went to the wardrobe to select a wool sweater from the dozen folded there. I chose a buttery-soft and blessedly warm scarlet cashmere sweater to replace my lightweight cotton top, and sent a silent word of gratitude to Tessa Gibbs for recognizing the vagaries of the English climate and providing for her guests accordingly.

I pulled on my hiking boots and started toward the door, then did an abrupt about-face and reached for the cell phone, knowing Bill would fret until he'd gotten his morning call. He was, as I'd expected, pleased to hear from me, but when I asked if there was any chance of him coming to my rescue in the near future, he hesitated.

"Have you looked outside yet?" he asked.

"No," I replied, "but I will now."

I went to the windows and pulled the heavy drapes aside. I squinted to protect my eyes from the painful glare of sunlight on snow, but I needn't have bothered — it was nearly as dark with the sun up as it had been with the sun down. The sky resembled an impenetrable block of lead, and although the wind had stopped battering the windowpanes, fat snowflakes continued to tumble lazily from the heavens.

"Oh," I said.

"Uh-huh," Bill confirmed.

"Doesn't look too promising, as far as rescues go."

"Nope."

I sighed. "Does anyone have any idea when this stupid storm will end?"

"The weathermen have lots of ideas," said Bill, "but since they failed to predict the storm in the first place, I'm reluctant to put too much faith in them."

He gave me a brief summary of activities on the home front — photos of Emma's snowbound horses had arrived via e-mail, attesting to a high level of equine health and happiness — as well as various catastrophes that had taken place around the world while I'd been away. As he moved from hotel fire to bus crash to earthquake, I realized, with a guilty twinge, how happy I was to be temporarily beyond the reach of television and radio.

"And those are the headlines for this morning," Bill concluded, mimicking the pompous tones of a professional announcer. "Stay tuned for further details. Rather, don't stay tuned." He reverted to his own voice. "We should probably stop the conversation here, Lori, in the interest of battery conservation."

"I'll call you at five," I promised.

"It might be better to save the phone for emergencies," said Bill.

"Being deprived of you could count as an emergency," I retorted.

"Now, Lori," Bill said firmly, "we don't know how long you'll be stuck there. I think that, from now on, you should call only if you need help. If I don't hear from you, I'll assume you're all right."

"Okay," I said with a sigh. "I think it's a terrible idea, but it's probably the sensible thing to do."

"It is. I love you," he added, and rang off.

I placed the cell phone on the bedside table and returned to the window to gaze morosely at the courtyard. A few cobbles had been swept clean by the wind, but most were covered by undulating drifts of snow, like swales on a golf course, and the outbuildings were buried nearly to their roofs.

"Not fit for man nor beast," I muttered.

The cliché brought Catchpole — and his budgies — to mind. I felt a vague sense of unease as I recalled his decision to return to his cottage after guiding me to my bedroom the night before. The snowdrifts were daunting enough in dim daylight. They would have been downright life-threatening in the dark.

I lifted my gaze to the snow-covered landscape beyond the courtyard, then hastily collected my down jacket, stocking cap, and gloves.

"If Catchpole hasn't shown his face by the time I finish breakfast," I told Reginald, "I'm going to go look for him."

I arrived in the kitchen to find Jamie standing over the range, stirring a heavy saucepan full of bubbling oatmeal. He was wearing the same dark blue sweater and faded jeans he'd worn the day before and his smile was as fetching as ever, but his face was drawn and his brown eyes were clouded with fatigue.

“Good morning,” he called. “Sleep well?”

“Very,” I said, piling my outdoor gear on the white dresser. “How about you?”

He shrugged. “Not as well as I’d hoped. The silence kept me awake.”

“I know what you mean,” I said, with a sympathetic nod. “Fortunately, it had the opposite effect on me.”

Steam rose from the brown teapot sitting on the scarred oak table, where a place had been set for one. Jamie gestured for me to take a seat.

“Wendy found porridge, sultanas, and a supply of long-shelf-life milk in the larder,” he informed me. “Hungry?”

“I could eat my boots,” I told him.

Jamie chuckled. “With or without sugar?”

“Either way,” I replied.

I sat at the table and poured a cup of tea for myself while Jamie spooned a generous helping of oatmeal into a bowl, sprinkled it with dried sultanas, and carried it to the table.

“Dig in,” he said, placing the bowl before me. “Wendy and I have already eaten our fill.”

“Where is Wendy?” I asked, starting in on the oatmeal.

"Up in her room, revising her trip." Jamie covered the saucepan and placed it on a trivet, then sat across the table from me and refilled his own teacup. "The blizzard upset her best-laid plans, apparently. I suspect that her floor's carpeted with maps by now."

"Huh," I grunted between spoonfuls. "I have a friend who's map-crazy. She could carpet St. Paul's Cathedral with her collection."

"I'm not a map person, myself," Jamie admitted. "I don't mind getting lost. To tell you the truth, I've come across some of my favorite places by getting lost."

"Me, too," I exclaimed, after a hurried gulp.

I regarded him fondly, knowing I'd found a hiking soul-mate, and told him about a superb pub I'd discovered at the top of a hill in a village that had turned out to be a mile east of my original destination. He came back with a story about a beautiful, abandoned church tucked away in a pocket valley he'd stumbled into by accident. By the time we finished swapping lost-traveler's tales, I'd consumed two brimming bowls of oatmeal and four cups of tea.

"I'm glad Wendy's in her room," I said.

"She's the kind of person who looks at a breathtaking landscape and sees *topography.* She wouldn't understand the joys of getting lost."

"You're not planning on getting lost today, are you?" Jamie glanced toward the white dresser. "I couldn't help but notice that you brought your jacket down with you."

I followed his gaze and felt a sting of self-reproach. I'd been having so much fun dancing down memory lane that I'd forgotten about Catchpole. Jamie responded to my urgent inquiry by saying that he'd seen neither hide nor hair of the old man all morning.

"In that case, I'd better be on my way." I pushed my chair back from the table and stood.

"Where are you going?" said Jamie, getting to his feet.

"To look for Catchpole," I said. "I'm worried about him. He's not exactly a spring chicken, you know, and he went into that storm all by himself last night, without his gun. Anything might have happened to him. I want to make sure he made it to his cottage in one piece."

"Are you sure it's wise to go out there on your own?" Jamie said doubtfully.

"I'm not afraid of him, if that's what you mean," I responded. "He won't hurt me, Jamie. He won't even threaten me. He's terrified of my powerful lawyer husband, remember?"

"I remember," Jamie said, "but I still don't like the thought of you going out there unescorted. I'll come with you."

"You will not," I said flatly. "Look at you. You have circles under your eyes and you nearly fell asleep when I was telling you about the overgrown graveyard I found in North Wales. You're in no condition to slog through snow, whereas I'm fit as a puppy."

"All right," Jamie said reluctantly. "If you insist on going alone, I can't stop you. But . . . wait here a minute, will you? I'll be right back."

He set off at a trot down the service corridor. While he was gone, I washed the dishes and kept watch through the Gothic windows for any sign of Catchpole. I saw nothing but snow, snow, and more snow. I was drying my hands on a tea towel I'd found in the white dresser when Jamie returned, carrying his blue parka.

"Take this," he said, draping the bulky garment over my shoulders. "Your jacket's not designed to cope with brutal weather."

"Thanks." I slipped my arms into the overlong sleeves and did up the zipper, then spread my arms wide and turned in a circle. "If I do get lost, I can use your parka as an emergency shelter."

"It is a bit large," Jamie conceded, "but it'll keep you warm, and that's the important thing."

While I put on my hat and gloves, Jamie told me how to find Catchpole's cottage.

"He pointed it out to me while he was frog-marching me from the mausoleum to the house," Jamie said. "Go straight back from the kitchen door, across the courtyard, to an open passageway between the outbuildings. When you reach the end of the passage, you'll see a clump of pine trees on your left. Catchpole's cottage is among the trees. You can't miss —"

I clamped a gloved hand over his mouth.

"Don't say it," I snapped. "Don't even *think* of saying it."

"Mmmph," Jamie agreed, nodding earnestly.

"If I'm not back by dinnertime, send out the dogs." I flashed him a jaunty smile and headed for the courtyard door, hoping fervently that I'd moved fast enough to ward off the travelers' curse.

Ten

The moment I set foot in the courtyard it became clear to me that Jamie's gallant gesture, though well-intentioned, had been unnecessary. The air was warmer outside than it had been in Ladythorne's frigid corridors. The blasting wind had dwindled to a vagrant breeze, and the flakes spiraling down from the gloomy sky struck my face like wet kisses instead of sharp needles.

I was grateful for the respite, but a glance at the gravid clouds told me that the situation could turn on a dime, so I didn't dawdle. I tried to keep to the spots that had been scoured bare by the wind, but they were too few and far between to serve as reliable stepping stones. More often than not, deep drifts got in my way, forcing me to employ an awkward, high-stepping gait that reminded me of my sons' first teetering steps.

Depth perception was a problem, too, because of a curious absence of shadows. The sun must have been lurking somewhere in the sky, but its beams had been severely blunted by the heavy overcast. Snow that should have been blindingly white was instead a uniform, pale gray. The diffused light robbed the drifts of contours and made it tricky to guess whether my next stumbling step would land me up to my ankles in snow, or up to my knees.

If there were few shadows, there were even fewer sounds. I strained to hear a single note of birdsong but heard only the gentle soughing of the wind, the occasional muffled thud of snow shivered loose from a tiled roof, and my own labored breathing. Frost had put a crust on the drifts, and each ungainly step was accompanied by a satisfying crunch that seemed unnaturally loud.

The open-air passageway between the low-roofed outbuildings was clogged by deeper drifts. I plowed through them by main force, dragging one leg, then the other, less afraid of falling than of catching a toe on Catchpole's buried body. He might not be my favorite person in the world — I couldn't quite forgive him for roughing up Jamie — but no one deserved to meet such a frosty fate.

I trembled to think of the old man making the journey from the abbey to his cottage in total darkness during the height of the storm. The howling wind would have snuffed out his oil lamp in the blink of an eye, and the plummeting snow would have obliterated every landmark. As I struggled onward, I wished with all my heart that I'd had the presence of mind the previous evening to persuade the old fool to stay put and let his budgies fend for themselves for one night.

When I reached the end of the passageway, I paused to give my gasping lungs a chance to recover, looked to my left, and saw a clump of towering pines that stood out like sentinels against a backdrop of leafless trees. The pines were so heavily burdened with snow that their lowest branches drooped to the ground, but they'd served as a windbreak, keeping the path that wound between them free from drifts.

I gladly left the difficult passage behind and made my way to the shelter of the trees. I'd gone no more than ten paces along the winding path when I caught sight of Catchpole's cottage.

The cottage itself was adorable — small, thatch-roofed, and built of golden limestone that had gone gray with the passage of time — but its fairy-tale prettiness was brought down to earth by a higgledy-piggledy agglomeration of sheds and lean-tos that looked as though they'd been cobbled together using warped timber and rusty metalwork scavenged from a junk yard. If the pine grove hadn't been there to act as a windbreak, the blizzard would have smashed into the frail buildings like a wrecking ball, leaving scattered piles of debris in its wake. I thought it a small miracle that they were still standing in any case, considering the amount of snow that had accumulated on their rickety roofs.

Tessa Gibbs, I thought, must have been thankful for the screen of needled branches that tastefully concealed Catchpole's attempts at low-budget carpentry from view, but I admired his ingenuity. Lucasta DeClerke hadn't made it easy for the old man to earn a living, so he'd done the best he could with what little he had.

Elation surged through me when I saw a steady stream of smoke rising from the cottage's chimney, and I sped up the path to knock on the front door. Although the smoke seemed to indicate that Catchpole hadn't perished in the blizzard, I wanted to see him with my own eyes before returning to the abbey. I was somewhat disappointed, therefore, when he responded to my knock without opening the door.

"Who is it?" he bellowed through the time-darkened wood.

"Lori Shepherd," I bellowed back.

"What do you want?"

"Um . . . nothing, really." I stood there like an expectant trick-or-treater, and when the door remained determinedly shut, added lamely, "I was worried about you."

"Why?"

I rolled my eyes in exasperation. "Oh, you know . . . hypothermia, frostbite, *wolves.* I wanted to make sure you were okay and I guess you are, so I won't bother you anymore. Have a nice day."

I loaded the parting line with sarcasm, and was about to turn on my heel and stomp back down the path when the door swung open and Catchpole appeared, clad in canvas dungarees, work boots, a plaid flannel shirt, and a moth-eaten, baggy brown cardigan.

"Come in," he said shortly. "I'll put the kettle on."

I nodded stiffly and followed him into a dimly lit parlor. It smelled of herbs and wood smoke and had the comfortably jumbled feel of a room furnished with castoffs — nothing matched, but everything went together. Faded rag rugs covered the flag-stone floor, an old patchwork quilt lay atop an oak chest, and a row of hunting prints in rustic frames hung above a sturdy oak desk. A six-shelf bookcase stood beside the desk, crammed with a dog-eared collection of biographies, travelogues, and books on natural history.

Dried herbs hung in bunches from the rafters, and fresh ones grew in clay pots clustered on the deep sill of the parlor's only window. A sagging easy chair and a wooden rocker sat facing the blackened stone hearth, where a log fire snapped and hissed. The chunky mantel shelf held assorted odds and ends — a tobacco jar, a pipe rack, a George IV coronation mug — and a wooden perch behind the rocking chair held a stuffed owl that nearly startled the life out of me when it slowly opened one enormous yellow eye.

"It's . . . not stuffed," I managed, pointing a shaky finger at the owl.

" 'Course it's not," said Catchpole. He seemed shocked by the very idea. "What would I want a stuffed bird for? Nasty things, if you ask me." He walked over to stroke the owl's back. "She's a long-eared owl, she is. See the tufts? Found her three weeks ago, her legs all tangled up in fishing line some fool left by the river. Cut her pretty deep, but she's on the mend. Got a pair of bluetits in the kitchen, fell out of their nest last spring. Don't seem to want to leave." He motioned for me to be seated in the easy chair. "Take off your coat. I'll see to the tea."

I gazed in fascination at the owl's tufted ears and mottled brown feathers, but she'd evidently lost interest in me because the yellow eye closed again, as slowly as it had opened. When the old man had gone to the kitchen, I chuckled softly. Only Catchpole, I suspected, would use the word *budgie* to describe such a supremely dignified wild creature.

I hung Jamie's parka over the back of the easy chair and stood close to the fire, in an effort to dry my snow-dampened jeans. A framed photograph sat on the mantel shelf, between the pipe rack and the coronation mug. It was a sepia-toned portrait of a little girl in a low-waisted, frilly white dress. She was sitting on a velvet pouffe, with one leg curled beneath her, and her long blond hair hung in sausage curls from a starched white bow. Her hands were folded primly in her lap, but her eyes twinkled with mischief and an enchanting smile graced her lips.

"Cream and sugar?" Catchpole called from the kitchen.

"Yes, please," I replied, noticing for the first time that the caretaker had stopped addressing me as "madam." Formality might apply in the big house, but in Catchpole's cottage, it seemed, we were on equal footing.

"Here you are, Mrs. Shepherd." Catchpole returned to the parlor carrying two large, blue-and-white striped mugs. He handed one to me, then sat in the rocking chair.

I wondered briefly whether I should explain to him that I hadn't changed my name when I'd married, and that while my husband was Bill Willis, I remained irrevocably Lori Shepherd, but gave it up as a lost cause.

"Please, call me Lori," I said, as I lowered myself into the easy chair. "Not just here, but in the abbey as well. I'm not used to being *madam*'ed. It makes me feel like a snooty old matron."

"Lori it is, then." Catchpole rocked in silence for a moment before continuing, "It was kind of you to think of me, Lori, but you had no cause to worry. I could find my way to the cottage under water, if need be."

"I'm a mother, Catchpole," I said. "It's my job to worry. I would have been much happier if you'd stayed at the abbey last night."

"That's as may be," he said stiffly, "but I wouldn't have been very happy. I don't fancy being laughed at, Lori, and that's what you were doing, you and the other two, laughing at me behind my back when I went to find milk for your tea."

I cast my mind back to the pertinent moment and decided that a diplomatic half truth was in order. "We weren't laughing at you, Catchpole. We were . . . laughing with joy. Because we survived the storm, you know? And your shotgun."

Catchpole reddened. "Less said about that the better."

"Mum's the word." I warmed my hands on the striped mug and took a sip of the strong, sweet tea. "If you feel like coming to the abbey, please do. Everyone will be glad to see you." I meant well, but regretted the words as soon as they were out of my mouth. I glanced at Catchpole's wooden expression and hastened to remedy my faux pas. "Not that I'm in a position to invite you to a place that's more yours than mine, Catchpole, but —"

"I understand," he said graciously, "and

I'll bear it in mind."

I nodded gratefully and gazed into the fire, wishing I could burn logs in my bedroom grate instead of coal. Coal was efficient — it burned steadily and gave off plentiful warmth — but it didn't have the sweet fragrance of wood smoke or fill the room with friendly snaps and crackles.

"I can see why you'd want to stay here, though," I said, after a time. "Your cottage is beautiful."

"You think so?" Catchpole sounded faintly puzzled. "Never thought of it like that. It's just home."

"That's what makes it beautiful." I raised my mug to the photograph on the chunky mantel shelf. "Is that your mother?"

"It's Miss DeClerke, when she was little," Catchpole informed me. "Mother was fond of the picture, so I keep it there, in memory of both of them."

I stood to take another look at the girl's bright eyes and enchanting smile. It was easy to imagine her clambering through Catchpole's maze of sheds and lean-tos, toasting crumpets over his open fire, or playing hide-and-seek with him among the pines.

"Did she spend much time here?" I asked.

"She did when she was a lass," said Catchpole, "but not so much by the time I came along. She was eleven years older than me, and it wouldn't have been proper for her to spend time here once she'd grown into a fine young lady. In the old days, there was more of a line drawn between servants and their employers."

"Do you miss the old days?" I asked.

"Sometimes," he admitted. "Things were slower back then, none of this rushing around that tires you out and gets you nowhere. People were more content to be who they were. No one wants to be himself, these days. Always trying on different skins, then wondering why they don't fit. It makes for a lot of unhappiness. And" — his gruff voice became taut — "you could trust people, back then. Didn't have to watch 'em like a hawk every minute of every day to keep 'em from robbing you blind."

I sensed another bout of Thieving Yank Fever coming on and returned to my chair. "Catchpole," I pleaded, "what can I do to convince you that I have no intention of taking so much as a soup spoon from the abbey?"

"You don't have to convince me," said Catchpole. "I've been told that you're who you say you are, but what about the other two? Who are they? No one seems to know."

I kept my expression carefully neutral as I silently reviewed Catchpole's comments. As far as I could tell, there was no one else in the cottage, and I seriously doubted that anyone who knew me had dropped in for a spot of tea and gossip in the midst of the blizzard. Was the old man hearing voices — the kind no one else could hear?

"Who told you about me?" I asked cautiously.

"Miss Gibbs's personal assistant," he replied. "Rang her on my mobile this morning. She vouched for you, but she'd never heard of the other two."

"You have a mobile phone," I said, with a sigh of relief.

" 'Course I do. Have to report in to Miss Gibbs, don't I? Tell her how the work is coming on, how the chars are doing, what supplies I need. Besides, Miss Gibbs didn't think I should be out here on my own without one. Something to do with insurance." He shrugged, as if dismissing the foolish concerns of the modern world, then leaned forward and returned to his original point. "It's not you I'm worried about, Lori. It's Mr. Macrae and Miss Walker."

"Why?" I asked, wondering what had rekindled the old man's paranoia.

"I told the three of you not to wander," he reminded me. "So I was a bit put out when I saw a light moving around inside the abbey last night."

"It was probably me and Jamie," I said. "I'm sorry. I know you wanted us to stay in our rooms, but it was too early to go to bed, so we spent an hour or so in the library, sitting and talking. Or you may have seen Wendy's light. She was roaming around for a while, looking for extra blankets, but she ended up in the library, too."

"The light I saw wasn't in the library," Catchpole intoned. "It was in the attics."

"The attics?" I repeated, frowning. "You saw a light moving in the attics?"

"The attics take up the whole of the top floor," Catchpole said. "And someone was up there last night."

I sat in silence while my mind went into overdrive. Neither Jamie nor I had wandered from our assigned floor the night before, but I couldn't be sure about Wendy. She'd arrived at the library long after I'd found Jamie there. If she'd spent the intervening time looking for blankets in the attics, she hadn't mentioned it to me.

"How do you get up to the top floor?" I asked.

"There's a panel in the wall at the head of the main staircase," said Catchpole. "Push on it and it pops open. You'll find the attic stairs behind it."

I nodded decisively. "Leave it with me. I'll find out who went up those stairs and why. I'm sure there's a perfectly innocent explanation."

"Going to question those two? Those two we know nothing about? What if you find out that they aren't so innocent?" Catchpole sat back in the rocker and regarded me shrewdly. "Have a care, Lori. You know how it is with cornered beasts. As often as not, they go for your throat."

Eleven

My second crossing of Ladythorne's arctic tundra wasn't as onerous as the first had been. I'd already broken a path through the worst of the drifts, and I was energized by a vision of the dry trousers awaiting me in my wardrobe at journey's end. Even so, I was extremely pleased to finally reach the courtyard door, brush snow from the big blue parka, and let myself into the warm kitchen.

I smiled when I saw Jamie. He was dozing in a Windsor chair he'd drawn close to the range, his chin on his chest, a book open in his lap. My overtired protector had evidently decided that his need for a comfortable bed was less pressing than his desire to witness my safe return. I was touched by his noble sacrifice and tried to cross the kitchen without waking him, but my attempt to tiptoe quietly in hiking boots proved to be an exercise in futility.

Jamie sat up, blinking, then rubbed his eyes and gave me a stern look.

"I was about to send out the dogs," he

informed me, and tapped his watch like a disapproving father. "It's past noon. You've been gone for *three hours.*"

"You think it's a stroll in the park out there?" I retorted. "It must've taken me the better part of forty-five minutes to get to the cottage, and coming back wasn't a cakewalk, either." I shook the snow from my cap and gloves, piled them atop my jacket, hung the parka on the back of a chair to dry, and crossed to stand before Jamie, adding contritely, "But I'm sorry if I worried you. Truly, I am. It was good of you to wait for me."

"Yes, well . . ." Jamie grumbled. "Just don't let it happen again." He closed the book and ran a hand over his face, as if he were still trying to wake up. "Did you find Catchpole?"

"I found him, and he's safe and sound, thank goodness." I turned to hold my cold hands over the range. "I don't know how he managed it. You could lose a small town in some of those drifts. He must be as tough as an old tree root."

"Was he happy to see you?" Jamie asked.

"I think he was more surprised than anything," I replied. "He gave me a cup of tea, though, and a chance to catch my breath."

"I'm glad to hear it," said Jamie. "I expected him to greet you with an angry shout and a waving fist. A cup of tea is much more civilized. What's his place like?"

"Homey," I said and left it at that. I felt I'd been given a privileged glimpse into Catchpole's private domain; to discuss it with Jamie seemed uncomfortably close to betraying a confidence. "What are you reading?"

"It's a book I found in the library." Jamie held the calf-bound volume out for my inspection. "It's about the Franklin Expedition."

My eyebrows rose. "You're reading about Sir John Franklin?" I said. "The arctic explorer?"

"The breadth of your knowledge leaves me speechless," Jamie declared.

"I could say the same about your choice of reading matter," I said. "You should be reading about sun-drenched beaches in Tahiti, not about an expedition that lost its way in the frozen wastes and was never seen again." I clucked my tongue. "No wonder you were fretting about me."

"Perhaps you'd help me chose a new title?" Jamie suggested. "I'm up for another visit to the lib—" He broke off midsyllable as Wendy came bustling in from the service corridor. "Hello, stranger," he said brightly. "Have you finished laying out a new route for your hiking trip?"

"Not yet," Wendy replied.

She was wearing a pair of loose black leggings and the pale-gray hand-knit sweater she'd worn the day before. She'd used a tortoiseshell clip to hold her long gray hair in place at the nape of her neck, and she'd swapped her heavy hiking boots for a pair of soft-soled slipper socks.

"You've been drudging away up there all morning," Jamie teased. "What's taking so long?"

"There are more options than I'd anticipated," said Wendy. "It'd help if I had a master map, but I can't find mine. I must have left it at home."

"What a shame," I said, though inside I was crowing. There was nothing more galling to a member of the map-and-compass crowd than the discovery that an essential map had gone astray. It forced them to contemplate the humiliating and terrifying prospect of *getting lost.*

Wendy must have detected an undertone of insincerity in my voice because she gave me a jaundiced look and subjected my snow-soaked jeans to a prolonged up-and-down stare.

"What have you been doing?" she asked. "Rolling around outside? Aren't you a little old to be playing in the snow?"

I bristled and was on the verge of a snippy comeback when Jamie stepped in.

"Lori's been on a mission of mercy, to confirm that Catchpole survived his journey home last night," he said. "She's been to his cottage and back, a feat the great Sir John Franklin himself would have lauded."

"Better you than me." Wendy dismissed me with a contemptuous glance and turned back to Jamie. "I'm hungry. Are you ready for lunch?"

"I'm sure we all are," Jamie said pointedly.

"I'll see what I can find in the larder," Wendy said, and went back into the service corridor.

I waited until she was out of earshot to murmur thoughtfully, "Do you think she'd be very upset if *all* of her maps went missing? It could be arranged."

"Never mind," said Jamie, laughing. "Go up and change out of those wet clothes. We'll have a pot of soup simmering on the range when you come down."

I smiled ruefully, collected my gear, and set out for my room. I heard Wendy rummaging in the larder as I passed, but didn't pause to look in. The less contact I had with her, I told myself, the better.

I was certain that she was responsible for Catchpole's mysterious light in the attics, and I didn't have many doubts about what she'd been doing up there. It was a long way to go for extra blankets, I reasoned, but a great place to search for something valuable to steal. How often did anyone inventory the odds and ends stashed in an attic? Ladythorne's were probably filled to the brim with priceless knickknacks. It would be ages before anyone noticed that some of them were missing.

They'd have to be small items, of course, small enough to be carried in a backpack, but I could think of dozens of portable treasures the DeClerke family might have accumulated over the years: snuff boxes, tankards, candlesticks, carriage clocks — the possibilities were endless.

I'd decided on the way back from Catchpole's cottage to keep my thoughts to myself until I'd had a chance to explore the attics on my own. Jamie had pooh-poohed my earlier misgivings as an oversensitive response to Ladythorne's eerie atmosphere. I wanted to have something concrete to show him this time — a recognizable boot print in the dust, perhaps, or a jimmied lock bearing the telltale scars of a short-handled pry bar. If I could prove to Jamie that Wendy had been sneaking around behind our backs, he'd have to take me seriously. He might even be willing to help me keep an eye on her.

I entered my bedroom, called a cheery hello to Reginald, and piled my jacket, hat, and gloves on the slipper chair. The room had grown chilly in my absence, so I dumped the rest of the coal on the fire and placed the empty scuttle near the door, making a mental note to take it downstairs for a refill.

The wardrobe yielded a lovely pair of charcoal-gray gabardine trousers as well as a pair of doeskin bedroom slippers I'd overlooked the night before. The slippers were a bit loose and the trousers a bit long, but an extra pair of socks solved the first problem, and rolled-up cuffs solved the second.

To avoid a third, and more distressing, problem, I opened the blue journal and said, "Dimity?"

The familiar copperplate unfurled steadily across the blank page. *Good after-*

noon, Lori. I trust you slept well?

"Never better," I said, perching on the edge of the bed. "And I've had a very eventful morning. I went out to the old caretaker's cottage to check up on him, and guess what he told me."

I can't begin to imagine.

"He told me he saw a light in the attics last night," I said. "It wasn't me or Jamie — we were in the library. So it must have been Wendy's light he saw."

Ah, yes, the famous — or should I say infamous? — Wendy. I've been waiting to hear about her. There was a note of disapproval in your tone when you mentioned her last night. Am I to understand that she's unlikely to become a close friend?

"She's a smart-mouth," I said bluntly. "She can't resist the urge to needle me. And she's one of those impossible, good-at-everything people who make me feel like I have six thumbs and half a brain, which I wouldn't mind so much if she weren't so smug about it."

Smug, rude, and good at everything. How perfectly odious.

"It's okay," I said. "I've found a way to pay her back."

Do tell.

"I'm going to prove that she pilfered

something from the attics," I said. "I'm going up there after lunch to look for evidence."

How exciting! And if you find no evidence?

I made a wry face. "Then I'll just have to short sheet her bed. Wish me luck?"

All the luck in the world, my dear. I'm glad you're keeping busy.

"Never a dull moment," I said. "Talk to you later."

I look forward to it.

I returned the journal to the bedside table, draped my wet jeans over the back of the chair at the writing table, and left the room, coal scuttle in hand.

As I descended the main staircase I realized that my stomach felt as empty as the scuttle, and was forced to admit that Wendy Walker had at least one redeeming trait — if breakfast was any indication, she was a dab hand at foraging for food.

Wendy exceeded my wildest expectations by producing a paella for lunch. It was a camper's pared-down version of the dish, made with canned and packaged ingredients scrounged from the larder, but it was delicious nonetheless, flavorful and very filling. Jamie's halfhearted offer to reheat the remains of Catchpole's apricot compote brought forth groans and a suggestion that we save it for after dinner.

"I didn't think you two cared for the compote," I commented, as we cleared the table. "Neither of you ate more than a spoonful of it yesterday."

"Do you always keep track of how much people eat?" Wendy asked.

"I was concerned for you." I gave her a sly glance. "I thought you might have been upset by Catchpole's story about Miss DeClerke's bloodthirsty ghost. You looked startled when he mentioned it — afraid, almost."

"I haven't been afraid of ghosts since I was a child," said Wendy. "And even then I kept a baseball bat under the bed to deal with them."

"I liked the compote," Jamie put in, "but by the time Catchpole served it, I'd filled up on the risotto."

"You didn't eat much of the risotto, either," I pointed out.

"I'd already had more than my share of your picnic lunch," Jamie reminded me. "The cranberry muffins were nearly as big as my head." He rinsed the last dish, put it in the drying rack, and dried his hands on the tea towel. "What shall we do with the rest of the day? I believe you and I were going to the library, Lori, to find a book on sun-drenched beaches. Care to join us, Wendy?"

"No, thanks," she said. "I'm going to have a bath, followed by a long nap."

"A nap sounds good to me, too," I chimed in, avoiding Jamie's eyes. "Sorry, Jamie, but my polar expedition seems to be catching up with me."

"Thank heavens." Jamie drooped weakly against the sink. "I was hoping for a lie-down this afternoon, but I didn't want to disappoint you."

"I'm not disappointed," I told him. "And you need the sleep. The silence kept him awake last night," I explained to Wendy, "but instead of going back to bed this morning, he sat up in the kitchen, waiting for me to come back from Catchpole's."

"Like a baby-sitter," Wendy said, and the accompanying snigger seemed to imply that I needed one. "I'll probably skip dinner," she added, heading for the service corridor, "so don't bother to come and get me."

"Won't you be hungry again by then?" Jamie called after her.

"I've got plenty of snacks in my back-pack," she replied. "They'll hold me until breakfast."

"I hope she chokes on them," I snapped the moment she disappeared. "A *baby-sitter* . . ." I huffed angrily. "She just can't keep her snotty comments to herself."

Jamie shrugged. "Not everyone has your sweet nature, Lori."

"Sweet? Me? Hardly," I said, blushing. "But at least I don't fling insults into the air every chance I get. What's up with her, anyway? She was nice enough to me when we first got here, but she's been a brat ever since." I fell silent, caught my lower lip between my teeth, and looked thoughtfully at Jamie's soulful eyes and attractively tousled hair. "Maybe it's you. Maybe she's showing off in front of you — trying to make me look bad so she'll look better. Some women can turn awfully catty when a good-looking man's thrown into the mix."

"Nonsense," said Jamie. "If you ask me, she's simply frustrated because her trip was interrupted."

"If you ask me, she's a pain in the patoot," I muttered heatedly.

"Don't get yourself so worked up over her. You'll ruin your nap." Jamie pointed to my empty coal scuttle and took me by the hand. "Come on, Lori. We'll find the coal hole, refill your scuttle, and go upstairs together, thinking happy thoughts."

The image of Wendy Walker behind bars in a high-security prison brought a grim smile to my lips, but I said nothing of it to Jamie. It didn't strike me as the sort of happy thought he'd had in mind.

Twelve

Jamie insisted on carrying the heavy scuttle up to my room for me. He told me to knock on his door when I'd finished my nap, so we could keep our library date, then went to his own room to catch up on the sleep he'd missed the night before. I was fairly sure he'd be out like a light in under five minutes, but I waited fifteen before putting my head into the corridor.

The sound of running water drifted to me from the bathroom. When it stopped, I waited another few minutes to give Wendy time to make herself comfortable in the tub, then switched on my small flashlight and retraced my steps to the head of the main staircase, confident that no one would hear the faint whisper of my doeskin slippers brushing against the thick maroon carpet.

When I reached the stairs, I stood with my back to them, walked straight toward the opposite wall, and pressed a palm against the linenfold paneling. I had to jump out of the way when a spring-loaded door swung silently outward, revealing the landing of a broad, gray-carpeted staircase with a plain wooden handrail and white-washed walls. The stairs appeared to go down to the ground floor as well as up to the attics.

"Servants' stairs," I murmured, and remembered Catchpole telling me that he'd used the back way to show the others to their rooms. Wendy had probably taken note of the hidden door then and used it later to gain access to the staircase, hoping it would lead her to a burglar's paradise.

I threw a quick glance back up the corridor, then stepped onto the landing and pulled the spring-loaded door shut behind me. The stairwell was lit by a weak trickle of gray light filtering down from above, so I turned off my flashlight and began to climb, pausing from time to time to examine a series of framed movie posters that hung on the whitewashed walls. The posters didn't celebrate Tessa Gibbs's many cinematic triumphs, but classic British films from the forties and fifties.

Had Lucasta DeClerke collected movie memorabilia? I wondered. If she had, she'd shown good judgment. Although the posters' garish colors and lurid graphics were distinctly out of place in Ladythorne's somber setting, my experience in the world of collectibles told me that the collection as a whole was worth a small fortune.

I'd spent a fair amount of time crawling through the attics of great houses while hunting for old books, and I thought I knew what to expect at Ladythorne — a warren of gloomy store rooms piled high with trunks, hat boxes, discarded furniture, and bric-a-brac, with a few latticed windows set high in the walls for ventilation.

I was in no way prepared, therefore, for the fathomless expanse of white that met my eyes when I reached the top of the stairs. A spotless, modern passageway stretched away to my left and right, far beyond the furthest reaches of my flashlight's searching beam. The corridor was about four feet wide and seemed to run the entire length of the abbey, from the cloisters to the bell tower.

The passageway's walls were white, the dropped ceiling was white, and short-napped white carpeting covered the floor from wall to wall. The domed skylights set into the ceiling at regular intervals were framed in white and inset with frosted glass. The only break in the mind-numbing whiteness came from a matched set of aggressively simple silver door handles that protruded from the inner wall, suggesting doors that were otherwise invisible. The decor was sleek, anonymous, and revoltingly antiseptic — a minimalist nightmare — and I strongly doubted that Lucasta DeClerke had had anything to do with it.

The silence in the passageway was absolute — not the mere absence of sound, but its negation, as if the walls had been designed to deaden any noise that might penetrate the skylights. Unnerved by the opaque stillness, I turned to my left, opened the first door I came to, and stepped cautiously inside. The thin gray light flooded in behind me.

It took me a moment to get my bearings, but when I did, my eyes widened in disbelief. I was standing in what appeared to be a screening room. Thirty well-padded, leather-covered theater seats rose in ranks from a blank screen at the front of the room, and an oblong window in the rear wall revealed a row of movie projectors. Everything looked brand-new and very expensive.

"Tessa," I said aloud, and felt even more admiration for the actress than I'd felt before.

Tessa Gibbs had come up with a remarkably elegant solution to the eternal problem of how to have one's cake and eat it, too. She'd preserved Ladythorne as a period gem while at the same time claiming the least visible part of it as her own. The screening room was more than a rich woman's indulgence. Although it would undoubtedly provide pleasure for her guests, it would also allow Tessa to do the kind of homework required by her profession. The heavy soundproofing was a thoughtful touch — visitors who preferred quieter pastimes wouldn't be disturbed by the entertainment taking place on the top floor.

A smaller chamber adjacent to the screening room reminded me of Tessa's obsession with feeding her guests. It had been charmingly decorated to resemble a silver-leafed art deco theater foyer, complete with a vintage popcorn machine, a soda fountain, a fancy espresso-maker, and a glass-enclosed candy counter. Pork scratchings, I assumed, would be available only at very private screenings.

As I crept along the white corridor, opening doors, I began to wonder if Tessa Gibbs was planning to swap her starring roles for a stint behind the camera. How else to explain the editing room and the sound studio she'd installed? They were tools I associated with the director's trade, and I had no trouble envisioning a hard-driving film producer pounding his — or her — fists on the teak tables in the various conference rooms.

Whether in front of the lens or behind it, Tessa evidently had no intention of losing her lovely figure. The fitness room at the far end of the corridor could have been plucked from an exclusive health club, and the adjoining spa featured a sauna, a jacuzzi, and a pair of massage tables. I discovered a small dance studio, as well, with a sprung floor, a barre, and mirror-lined walls.

It wasn't until I reached the cloister end of the white passageway that I finally found something resembling a store room, but it was as clean and well-organized as a hospital warehouse. Its miscellany of items had been tagged and placed in strict numerical order on adjustable floor-to-ceiling metal shelves. I whipped out my flashlight and moved up and down the aisles, counting under my breath, but nothing appeared to be missing.

There wasn't a trace of dust on the white-tiled floor, either. If Wendy Walker had spent part of the previous evening prowling the store room, I couldn't prove it, nor could I prove that she'd taken anything. Forced to admit defeat, I plodded disconsolately past a row of dented lampshades, turned the corner into the central aisle, and let out a shriek that must have strained the soundproofing.

"Good God . . ." I clutched at my chest as the pale face hovering in the shadows came into sharper focus. "Don't *ever* do that to me again. I thought you were Lucasta's *ghost.* I could have had a *heart attack.*"

"Sorry," Jamie said, walking toward me. "I did call out in the doorway, but my voice didn't seem to carry."

"The walls absorb sound," I said, leaning limply against a metal shelf. "What are you doing here, anyway? You're supposed to be taking a nap."

"It's six o'clock, Lori," he said mildly. "I slept for two hours. I knocked on your door when I woke up and when you didn't answer, I looked in. You weren't in your room, so I went looking for you. I thought I might find you up here. The door in the wall was open."

"I closed it," I said.

"You must not have pulled hard enough," said Jamie. "It's a tricky latch. Catchpole had to put his shoulder to it last night when he took Wendy and me to our rooms." He cocked his head to one side. "Did he tell you about the servants' stairs?"

I nodded.

"And you decided to go exploring." Jamie grinned and clapped me on the shoulder. "I can't say that I blame you. How often does one get the chance to wander freely through a place like Ladythorne? This floor's full of surprises, isn't it? I think I saw a dance studio back there, and I wouldn't mind having a go at the sauna. . . ."

While Jamie rattled on, I hung my head in shame. His friendly chatter and generous assumptions made me feel very small indeed. If I'd caught Wendy Walker lurking in the store room, my first impulse wouldn't have been to congratulate her on her spirit of exploration.

"To tell you the truth, Jamie," I said, prodded by my guilty conscience, "I didn't come up here just to take a look around."

"No?" He waited patiently for me to go on.

"Can we go to the library?" I said, unable to meet his innocent gaze. "I don't feel comfortable up here. There aren't any books."

* * *

Jamie lit a fire in the library's stone hearth and sat in the leather armchair he'd occupied the night before. I sat opposite him, twisting my hands in my lap. He hadn't asked a single question on the way down from the attics. His forbearance made my guilty conscience cringe.

"The thing is, Jamie," I began haltingly, "Catchpole told me that he saw a light moving in the attics last night. I automatically assumed that Wendy had gone up there to" — I cleared my throat — "steal something."

"Pardon?" said Jamie. "I didn't hear the last bit."

"I thought she'd gone up there to steal something," I repeated, raising my voice. "I wanted to prove to you that I was right about her, so I went looking for evidence. I didn't find any."

Jamie pursed his lips and turned his gaze to the fire. "Catchpole said he saw a light moving in the abbey, did he? How strange . . ."

"What's strange about it?" I asked.

"I have no wish to impugn Catchpole's integrity, but I'm not entirely convinced that he was telling you the truth." Jamie rested his elbows on the arms of his chair and tented his fingers. "The snow was falling so fast and hard yesterday that I couldn't see the abbey clearly until he'd shoved me into the courtyard — and the sun was still up, then. I don't believe he could have seen the abbey from his cottage through the snow, after dark." He tapped the tips of his index fingers together. "There's the pine grove to consider, as well. His cottage is surrounded by a heavy growth of pines, isn't it?"

"Yes," I said.

"The interlacing branches would block his view of the abbey even if the snow didn't," Jamie said. "I don't know how he could have seen a light moving in the attics."

"Why would he lie to me?" I asked.

"Maybe his eyes were playing tricks on him," Jamie suggested. "Or maybe it was his mind. We're talking about a man who spent fifty years working for a woman who was probably insane. He believes in ghosts and he spends a lot of time alone. He may believe what he told you, Lori, but it may not have been the truth as you and I know it."

I recalled the nostalgic photograph gracing Catchpole's mantel shelf, the injured owl perched behind his rocking chair, and the orphaned bluetits who'd taken up residence in his kitchen. He was an old man living with one foot in the past and animals as his closest companions. Perhaps he saw lights in the attics every night, whether they were there or not.

"Do you think he's nuts?" I said.

"Possibly." Jamie shrugged. "On the other hand, he may have deliberately misled you in order to stir things up for his own amusement. He certainly found a receptive audience."

I covered my face with my hands. "I know. I feel like such a jerk. I've been to the cottage. I've seen the pines with my own eyes. I should have realized that they'd block his view, but I was so eager to punish Wendy for being mean to me that I didn't stop to think. I just went off half-cocked, as usual." I groaned. "I have a horrible feeling that I should apologize to Wendy, but frankly, I'd rather eat ground glass."

"There's no need to apologize," Jamie soothed. "Least said, soonest mended." He stood. "Hungry? I'm not as skilled in the kitchen as Wendy, but I can be trusted to heat up a can of soup."

"Should we invite her to join us?" I asked.

"I already did," said Jamie, "and she refused. She's curled up in bed with a paperback and an enormous bag of trail mix. I don't think we'll see her again until morning."

"Good. I may be able to look her in the eye by then." I got to my feet. "You're a much nicer person than I am, Jamie. I've been acting like a petty-minded little punk. Thanks for not rubbing my nose in my stupidity."

"You're welcome." Jamie sidled closer to me. "You can show your gratitude to me in a more concrete way after dinner, if you like."

I opened and closed my mouth a few times before managing a much too casual "What did you have in mind?"

"A guided tour of the library," he replied. "I've been dying to plumb the depths of that repository of arcane knowledge you call a brain."

"You're on," I said, almost relieved that his interest in me was purely intellectual.

I stuck out my hand to shake his in a scholarly fashion, but when he raised it to his lips, I felt a flutter that was neither pure nor intellectual. As we went to our respective rooms to fetch our oil lamps, I told myself not to worry. If my natural impulses started to get out of control, I could always put in an emergency call to Bill.

We had a lovely evening. After hunting down the lamp room and refilling our oil lamps, we supped on bowls of coconut ginger soup scrounged from the larder and a bottle of chardonnay Jamie liberated from the wine cellar. The lamps' golden glow made the simple meal seem like a feast, and Jamie's delightful conversation distracted me from the depressing sight of snow falling with renewed vigor outside the Gothic windows above the sink.

We returned to the library in high spirits. Jamie had already done a fair amount of browsing and was filled with questions about the books he'd found. I showed him examples of tree-calf, marbled-calf, and mottled-calf bindings, and dazzled him with my knowledge of obscure Victorian writers. When he pointed to a marble bust sitting atop the map case, I promptly identified it as Tennyson.

"He's easy," I said, laying a hand on the poet laureate's noble brow. "Everyone knows what old Alfred looks like."

"Old Alfred," Jamie repeated, shaking his head. "You make it sound as if you play croquet with him every Tuesday."

I laughed. "Does Wendy know there's a

map case in here?"

"It wouldn't matter if she did," said Jamie. "The maps are out of date. They wouldn't help her revise her hike."

"You've looked through the map case, then," I said, and when Jamie nodded, asked archly, "Are you sure you've been through *all* of it?"

"I looked in each drawer," he said.

I winked at him, moved Lord Tennyson to the floor, and lifted the map case's hinged lid.

"Voilà!" I said with a flourish. "Most people focus on the drawers and miss the top compartment."

"I didn't realize it was there." Jamie came to look over my shoulder. "What's in it?"

I rifled through the thick sheaf of oversized sheets that had been stored in the hidden compartment. "Architectural drawings, floor plans, layouts of the grounds and gardens. Oh, look at this, Jamie." I slid a sketch of a rose bower from between the other sheets and held it up for him to see. "Beautiful, isn't it? I hope Tessa restores the gardens once she finishes with the house."

"After seeing what she's done to the attics, I'm not sure I want her to," Jamie commented. "I wouldn't mind if she restored the original Victorian plantings, but I'm afraid she might install one of those hideous modern gardens filled with concrete troughs and indescribable hunks of rusting sheet metal."

"Tessa wouldn't do that." I put the sketch back where I'd found it, closed the map case, and restored Tennyson to his perch. "She has too much respect for Ladythorne. That's why she hid the modern bits upstairs."

"I hope you're right," said Jamie. "I've never understood the appeal of concrete troughs."

He left the map case and opened the door of yet another glass-enclosed bookcase, but I hurried after him and put a restraining hand on his arm.

"Sorry," I said, "but the tour's over for now. I have to get some sleep. I wasted my nap time on a wild goose chase and I'm beat."

"All good things must come to an end, I suppose." Jamie closed his hand over mine. His dark eyes gleamed like pools of burgundy as he looked down at me and his honeyed voice grew husky as he said, "I've enjoyed this, Lori. I've enjoyed every moment I've spent with you. Truly."

"It's been fun for me, too," I said, a bit unsteadily. "It's been a long time since anyone *volunteered* to listen to me natter on about books."

"I could listen to you all night long," he murmured.

"Wow. You must have had an amazing nap." I took a trembling breath and gently slid my hand from his grasp. "I'll see you in the morning."

I retrieved my oil lamp and ordered my weak knees to carry me to my bedroom, leaving Jamie to bank the fire and trail slowly in my wake, looking like a little boy who'd lost his puppy.

Thirteen

I staggered into my room, closed the door, and stood stock-still, listening intently. When I heard Jamie's door swing shut across the corridor, I pressed a hand to my heaving breast and congratulated myself on a narrow escape.

The steamy look Jamie had given me in the library seemed to suggest that he was open to plumbing the depths of something other than my brain, but it wasn't him I was worried about. It was me. I found Jamie unspeakably attractive, on every level, and the late hour only magnified his charms. If my bedroom hadn't been so chilly, I would have contemplated a cold shower.

Instead, I busied myself with sweeping the mound of ashes from the hearth, building a fresh fire, and tidying the room. I put my jeans and outdoor gear in the wardrobe, moved my day pack from the slipper chair to the writing table, straightened the bedclothes, and drew the drapes.

When I ran out of busywork, I put Reginald and the oil lamp on the tea table and carried the blue journal with me to the plump armchair. After settling Reg in the crook of my arm, I placed the journal in my lap and opened it, hoping that a visit with Aunt Dimity would keep me from dwelling on those smoldering brown eyes.

"Dimity?" I said. A welcome sense of calm came over me as the familiar lines of royal-blue ink looped and curled across the page.

Good evening, Lori. Were you successful in your search for evidence?

I ducked my head in embarrassment and firmly pushed aside every farfetched suspicion I'd ever harbored about Wendy.

"I didn't find anything," I confessed, "because there wasn't anything to find. Catchpole was lying to me when he —" I broke off as Dimity's handwriting sprinted across the page.

Did I hear you correctly, Lori? Did you say Catchpole?

"Yes," I said. "He's the old caretaker. The one with the cottage? His family worked at Ladythorne for donkey's years, but he's the only one left now and I think he may be off his rocker. He held us all at gunpoint when we first got here, then he turned nice and helpful, then he lied to me about seeing the light in the . . ." I fell silent as Dimity's handwriting resumed.

Interesting. Most interesting. The writing paused, as if Dimity were digesting my comments, then continued. *Lucasta spoke to me of the Catchpole family. She told me that she missed them dreadfully and was longing for their return. It's incredible, and at the same time deeply touching, to learn that one member of the family still resides at the abbey, regardless of his eccentricities.*

The significance of Dimity's words was not lost on me. If she'd spoken with Lucasta, she must have known the woman personally, which meant that she could give me a reliable, firsthand account of Lucasta's behavior and character.

Grateful for the diversion, I sank more deeply into the plump armchair and focused my attention on recalling the strange tale Catchpole had told about Lucasta Eleanora DeClerke — granddaughter of Grundy and Rose, heiress to the family fortune, the last of the line, the broken-hearted bride-that-never-was, the plucky young woman who turned Ladythorne into a sanctuary for wounded soldiers and spent her last years on earth alone in one room, consumed with hatred, writing endless letters to America.

"You spoke with Lucasta DeClerke?" I said, emerging from my musings. "I thought she was a recluse. Did you know her?"

I met her on a few occasions. My commanding officer sent me up from London during the war, to collect information about British flying officers convalescing at Ladythorne Abbey. Lucasta wasn't a recluse in those days — quite the opposite. She was most hospitable. When I told her I was from Finch, she welcomed me as a neighbor. It was from her that I learned the history of the house and the DeClerke family. She made my days at the abbey among the most pleasant of the war.

The wind whistled outside the windows, and I looked up from the journal to stare into the fire, lost in thought. If I closed my eyes I could see the mischievous child in Catchpole's photograph grown into young womanhood. If I concentrated, I could see Dimity in her trim uniform, walking arm in arm with the bustling heiress, surveying the hospital beds dressed with the family linen, the nourishing meals served on the family china. Dimity would have been fascinated by the story of Grundy DeClerke's rise in the world, impressed by Lucasta's dedication, and grateful to find respite, however brief, from the dangerous, dark days of the Blitz.

"How old was Lucasta when you met her?" I asked.

She was nineteen, and I can vouch for the fact that she possessed a teenager's boundless energy. No job was beneath her. She lent a hand wherever it was needed, whether it was emptying bedpans or filling out reams of paperwork. I could scarcely keep up with her. She was sweetly pretty, too, and took great care always to dress smartly. The ward matron didn't approve, naturally, but Lucasta paid her not the slightest attention. She knew by instinct that the sight of a pretty girl can lift a wounded man's spirits, and dressed accordingly. She brought color, freshness, and gaiety to men who'd almost forgotten such things existed.

Lucasta seemed to come to life before me, tireless, cheerful, caring, and so very young. What brutal blow, I wondered, had transformed this scintillating creature, this beguiling gamine, into a shriveled hermit huddled in one room, living on tea and toast and hatred?

"What happened to her, Dimity? Why did she change?"

No one came through the war unchanged,

Lori. Lucasta had suffered heart-rending losses.

"So did you," I reminded her gently, "but you didn't let your suffering turn you into a hermit."

While it's true that my fiancé was killed in the war, my situation was different from Lucasta's. I was older when I lost Bobby than she was when she lost her young man. I'd led a less sheltered life. I was better prepared to carry on, despite my grief. And

I caught my breath when the handwriting stopped; after a moment, I gave a little sputter of exasperation. "Please don't leave me dangling, Dimity. Catchpole couldn't tell us what happened because he didn't know. Lucasta never confided in him or his parents. If you can fill in the blanks, please do."

I was about to add that I could cope with my losses better than Lucasta because I wasn't betrayed by those I served, as she was.

I shifted Reginald to my left arm and turned up the lamp's wick, the better to see Dimity's response to my next question.

"How was she betrayed, Dimity?"

I found out quite by accident. I was working late one night at headquarters and overheard a conversation between two high-ranking officers. Something had happened at Ladythorne

Abbey. A theft. Miss Lucasta DeClerke believed that one of the American officers then in residence at the abbey had stolen an extremely valuable family heirloom. It was a blanket accusation. She had no particular suspect in mind, but she wanted the culprit identified and brought to justice, and her property returned.

"But no one listened to her," I put in eagerly, as Catchpole's tale came rushing back. "Catchpole told us that the whole thing was hushed up, that the authorities brushed her off because they didn't want to provoke a diplomatic stink between allies so near the end of the war in Europe."

There was more to it than that, I'm afraid. Lucasta evidently hurt her case by withholding vital information. She offered no proof that the theft had taken place. She refused to show anyone where the stolen items had been kept, and she never retained a solicitor to represent her. Even if the military authorities had wanted to conduct an investigation at such a sensitive time, they had no way of collecting evidence or following leads.

I sighed. "I guess they couldn't just take her word for it."

I'm afraid not. I'm certain that their refusal to take her at her word compounded her sense of outrage. She'd welcomed those young men into her home. No doors were locked against them because she trusted them implicitly. When they betrayed her trust, she turned to the authorities for redress, and they, too, betrayed her. They shut down the convalescent home and left Lucasta to shake her fist at the wind. It was a sad and sorry end to what had been a happy and successful partnership.

I twiddled Reginald's ears absently and tried to imagine what Lucasta had felt at the happy partnership's ignominious demise. "I can understand the military keeping a lid on the incident, Dimity, but if I'd been in Lucasta's shoes, I'd have screamed it from every rooftop in London. At the very least, I'd've written an angry letter to the Times. Why didn't she go public?"

Her cries would have gone unheard. Consider the state we were in, Lori. We had far more pressing problems to deal with than an unsubstantiated theft in a remote country house. We were clearing the streets of rubble, rebuilding, trying to conceive of what life would be like without war. It was a year before I could sleep without blackout curtains, many more before I stopped reflexively scanning the night sky for bombers. Who would listen to the unproven complaints of a wealthy heiress when the rest of us were still queuing up at the butcher's with ration books, and when thou-

sands were still homeless?

"She must have felt utterly abandoned," I said, drawing Reginald closer. "Did she tell you what happened? Did she ask you for help?"

Lucasta refused to see me, speak with me, or have anything to do with me after her demands for justice were rebuffed. She cut me out of her life completely because I'd told her of my great friendship with your mother.

I put a hand to my forehead, remembering Catchpole's rants about thieving Yanks. "She cut you out because my mother was an American, and Lucasta had declared her own private war on the United States."

I'm afraid so. It's a great pity, but this final blow, coming upon so many others, drove Lucasta into a kind of obsessive madness from which she never emerged.

"What on earth was stolen?" I demanded. "What material possession could possibly be worth the price of her sanity?"

It was known as the Peacock parure.

"Sorry?" I squinted at the unfamiliar word. "What's a . . . *parure?*"

A parure is a matched set of jewelry. The Peacock parure was a particularly magnificent set: It consisted of a tiara, four bracelets, a choker, an elaborate necklace, two brooches, and a pair of earrings — an unparalleled display of the finest diamonds and the purest white gold. Grundy DeClerke bought the Peacock parure from an Indian prince and presented it to Lucasta's grandmother as a belated wedding gift when they gave their Jubilee ball. I like to think it was his way of thanking her for marrying him long before he'd made his fortune.

An image of Rose DeClerke took shape in my mind — the ostrich feathers waving languidly above the glittering tiara, the sturdy wrists graced with four spectacular bracelets, the daring neckline designed to display the waterfall of diamonds cascading from the choker encircling her neck.

"And the earrings were the size of my thumbnail," I murmured, and sat up excitedly. "I think I've seen it, Dimity. I think I've seen the Peacock parure. Not the real thing, but a photograph of it." I described the morocco-bound album Jamie had found in the library, the memento of the costume ball the DeClerkes had given in honor of Queen Victoria's Diamond Jubilee. "There were peacocks in the photo, too, so she must have been wearing the parure. Diamonds for the Diamond Jubilee," I concluded. "What could be more romantic?"

The parure became a cherished heirloom, Lori. It was given to Lucasta's mother on her wedding day, and Lucasta, in turn, would have received it on hers, had the happy day ever occurred. The Peacock parure wasn't simply a material possession, my dear. It was a symbol of everything Lucasta had lost — the past she'd shared with her father, the future she'd hoped to share with her husband. Its disappearance must have cut her to the quick.

"Then why didn't she cooperate with the authorities?" I asked, with a touch of asperity. "Why didn't she show them the hiding place? Why didn't she hire a lawyer? I mean, if her grandmother's jewels meant the world to her, why didn't she do everything she could to get them back? Unless . . ." My voice trailed off as a disturbing idea derailed my train of thought.

Dimity was a step ahead of me. *Unless the parure was never stolen. Unless Lucasta invented the theft for reasons of her own. Is that what you were about to say?*

"I'm not sure," I said. "Give me a minute."

I stared into the fire and tried to put myself in Lucasta's place. The war was winding down. The convalescent home was going to close no matter what I did. I'd already lost my father and my fiancé. Now I was losing what had become my mission in life. What would I do next?

"Could it be, Dimity?" I hesitated to speak because I couldn't quite believe what I was saying. "Is it possible that she . . . made the whole thing up? It would explain why she didn't hire a lawyer or produce any evidence for the authorities."

It would also explain why she never discussed the theft with those closest to her. Lucasta told me how fond she was of the Catchpoles, and you've told me that the family remained loyal to her for years, despite increasingly trying circumstances. Yet Catchpole himself admitted that he never knew what happened, nor did his parents. Why didn't she confide in them? The Catchpoles would have been her staunchest supporters.

"They probably would have stuck by her even if they'd known that the theft was nothing but a sick fantasy. But they might have treated her differently — with an undercurrent of pity, perhaps. They wouldn't have shared her outrage." I ran a hand through my hair in consternation. "Did Lucasta invent a robbery because she couldn't handle her real losses — including the loss of her wounded officers?"

The suspicion has crossed my mind from

time to time, over the years. I first met Lucasta only a few months after her father's shocking death. Considering the circumstances, I found her almost too bright, too cheerful. Everyone spoke of how brave she was, but I couldn't help wondering if she was concealing a great deal of anger behind her pretty smile. I couldn't be sure, of course. People sometimes are what they present themselves to be. In light of subsequent events, however, I believe my suspicions were well-founded. Suppressed anger, as you know, is like a time bomb. Sooner or later it's bound to explode, and God help those who are in its way when it does.

"She buried her grief in her work," I mused aloud, "and when her work ended, her grief ambushed her. She concocted a crazy story because she was furious with the world for taking away everyone she loved." The notion left me dazed and saddened. "The worst thing is, she fed off that rage for the rest of her life. The letters she wrote to America were probably filled with false accusations. Maybe she came to believe her own lies. It's so awful, Dimity."

Particularly awful for the accused, I should think. You do realize the implications of our new line of reasoning, don't you, my dear?

"Implications?" I pondered Dimity's question for a moment, then sat forward in the chair. "Are you suggesting . . ." I swept the room with a searching gaze. "Are you telling me that the Peacock parure is still hidden in Ladythorne Abbey?"

It wouldn't surprise me in the least if it were. If found, it would finally remove the taint of suspicion from those poor officers who bore the brunt of Lucasta's paranoid delusions. I suspect you were sent here for precisely that purpose.

I looked down at the journal with a perplexed frown. "No one sent me here, Dimity."

Come now, Lori — you were caught in a storm that wasn't forecast, placed on a path you'd no intention of taking, and led to a house you never knew existed. Do you truly believe you came here by chance?

"It's not all that unusual for me to take the wrong path," I put in, in the interest of truth.

Whether you came here by design or by accident, you've been given a puzzle to solve. I suggest you solve it. Find the Peacock parure, my dear. Prove to the world that those men were innocent.

Fourteen

I sat in befuddled silence as Dimity's words faded from the page. Any notion I'd had of sleep faded with them. It was as if she'd ordered me to don my armor and ride off in search of the Holy Grail. I liked the idea, but felt singularly ill-equipped to follow through on it.

I placed the journal on the tea table, planted my elbow on the arm of the chair, and cupped my chin in my hand. Ladythorne Abbey was no Blenheim Palace, but it still had dozens of rooms. The Peacock parure might be hidden in any one of them. It might even have been broken up and stashed in several different places — earrings here, bracelets there, tiara somewhere else. I had a hard time locating stray socks in my cottage and, compared to Ladythorne Abbey, my cottage was a scantily furnished nutshell.

"It's impossible," I muttered. "Dimity's asking too much."

A small avalanche of coals sent a welter

of sparks swirling up the chimney. As I knelt to add fuel to the fire, I felt Reginald's gaze on me. Glancing over my shoulder, I detected a reproachful gleam in his black button eyes, as if he were reminding me that Dimity had never asked too much of me before.

"Listen, Reg," I said. "The only good thing to come out of this whole conversation is that I've stopped thinking about Jamie. Apart from that, it's just plain ridiculous."

The gleam seemed to grow more reproachful.

"Okay, I'm listening." I sat cross-legged on the hearth rug and faced my bunny, who was comfortably ensconced in the slipper chair. "Give me one good reason to believe that it's not an absurdly impossible task."

As I contemplated the twin sparks of firelight reflected in Reginald's eyes, it slowly dawned on me that the task might not be as impossible as it seemed. According to Catchpole, Tessa Gibbs's army of workmen had spent the past two years renovating the abbey. They'd gutted the attics and thoroughly refurbished the rest of the house. They'd redone the electrical wiring, put in new plumbing, relaid the floors, and replaced miles of rotting wall panels. They'd had ample opportunity to discover any treasure-filled hidey-holes that might exist in the fabric of the house. With the eagle-eyed Catchpole watching them as closely as he watched the charwomen, they couldn't have kept such a discovery secret, and if Tessa Gibbs had suddenly come into possession of something as valuable as the Peacock parure, her lawyer — my husband — would have known about it and mentioned it to me.

"What it boils down to, Reg, is this," I said. "We've limited the search. I wouldn't have to tear walls apart or pry up floorboards to find the parure." I glanced at the marquetry writing table. "It must be hidden in a piece of furniture — in a secret drawer or a concealed compartment of some kind."

Reginald's eyes glowed with encouragement. He seemed to think I was on the right track, so I kept going.

"Catchpole told me that some of the rooms aren't finished yet. He said" — I frowned with the effort of recalling his exact words — "some of the furniture was pretty rough. Which means that some of the abbey's furniture hasn't been refinished or reglued or generally messed about. It's as it was when Lucasta was alive."

I hugged my knees to my chest as my plan began to take shape. I'd find the rooms with the shabbiest furniture and start from there. If necessary, I'd move on to search the furnishings in the renovated rooms. It wouldn't be an easy job, but at least it was feasible.

"Thanks for the help, Reg." I reached out to shake my bunny's paw. "The needle may still be pretty miniscule, but the haystack's not as enormous as I thought it was."

I checked my watch. It was half past ten. If I waited until morning to begin my search, I'd have to manufacture excuses for rambling through the house alone. It would be much better to start at once, while Catchpole was in his cottage and my two housemates were asleep.

I turned the wick down low on the oil lamp to give the impression that I'd gone to bed, then took the small flashlight from the pocket of my gabardine trousers and tiptoed noiselessly into the corridor. My first stop, I decided, would be the library. Before commencing my search for shabby furniture, I wanted to feast my eyes once more on my Holy Grail.

* * *

The flashlight's slender beam shot ahead of me as I entered the library. There was a faint trace of warmth in the room, but little light — the banked fire had burned down to cherry-red embers. Again I was aware of the heavy silence that hung over the abbey, lying deep in its hidden valley, cocooned in a mantle of snow. Even the garrulous pilgrims in the Canterbury mosaic seemed subdued, as if they'd agreed to stop swapping stories and settle in for the night. I paused briefly to admire their muted beauty, then directed the flashlight's beam toward the table beside the chair Jamie had been using. I saw at once that the Jubilee photograph album was no longer where Wendy had left it the night before.

I checked the other tables in the room, found nothing, and swung the flashlight toward the bookshelves. It seemed reasonable to assume that Jamie had put the album back where he'd found it. If he had, I'd have no trouble tracking it down. I might be pig-ignorant when it came to Victorian ranges, but I knew my way around books.

I skipped over the shelves Jamie and I had examined during our tour and moved on to a glass-enclosed bookcase we hadn't opened. It was devoted exclusively to photograph albums. All were bound in the same sumptuous morocco that covered the Jubilee album, with fine paper labels affixed to the spines. The small, precise handwriting on the labels proclaimed each album's date and general contents: family picnics, christenings, house parties, balls, funeral processions, birthdays, patriotic celebrations. If the labels were accurate, the albums contained an intriguing visual history of family life in Victorian and Edwardian England. Nothing would have pleased me more than to spend the rest of the night exploring the vanished worlds captured in those antique images.

Instead, I breathed a short sigh of frustration. The Jubilee album was missing. A gap yawned on the shelf where the album should have been, the only gap in the collection. I opened the glass doors and bent low, to make sure the album hadn't accidentally been thrust to the back of the shelf. It wasn't there.

As I closed the doors, the flashlight's reflected beam shot straight into my eyes. I squinted, then blinked away the after-spots, peevishly reminded of Wendy's cyclopean head lamp. Then I stopped blinking.

"Wendy," I said aloud, and gazed into the polka-dotted darkness as all of the vague suspicions I'd pushed aside came flooding back.

Had Wendy taken the album? The question seemed absurd on the face of it. Wendy had claimed to be repulsed by old photographs. "Old photographs give me the creeps," she'd said, but that was exactly what she would have said if she'd been feigning disinterest.

Had she pretended to ignore the Jubilee album in order to downplay its importance, then come back to retrieve it from the library after Jamie and I had gone? Why would she want to study the photographs in private? Why would the Jubilee album hold a special significance for her, unless she somehow knew about the Peacock parure?

"How in the world could she know about the parure?" I muttered under my breath, and padded silently across the Turkey carpet to stand in the circle of warmth given off by the glowing embers.

Since I was pretty sure that Aunt Dimity was not on speaking terms with Wendy Walker, it seemed safe to assume that Wendy had obtained her information from a more conventionally human source. But who, besides Aunt Dimity, would have the inside scoop on the parure? Not even

Catchpole was aware of its importance. I cast my mind back to the conversation Wendy and I had shared in the library the night before, and the wheels of logic began to turn in earnest.

During the course of our somewhat stilted tête-à-tête, Wendy had described her father as a marksman. *Marksman* was a common military term. What if Wendy's father had been a soldier, I asked myself, and not just any soldier, but one of the wounded Americans Lucasta had unjustly accused of theft? It went without saying that he would have declared his innocence to his daughter. He would have explained to her that no one had taken the fabulous parure, would perhaps have shown her the abusive letters Lucasta had sent to him after the war. And years later, the protective, clever, and bitterly resentful daughter would arrive "by accident" at a virtually uninhabited Ladythorne Abbey, equipped to break and enter and *take revenge* on the woman who'd slandered and tormented her father.

The blizzard must have complicated her plans. Wendy couldn't have anticipated the arrival of two genuine castaways at Ladythorne Abbey. I was certain that, if she hadn't been saddled with me and Jamie,

Wendy would have dealt with Catchpole by bashing him over the head with her pry bar.

I clapped a hand to my forehead as I recalled the pristine blanket of snow that had covered the staircase leading to Ladythorne's main entrance. I understood, now, why there'd been no footprints. Wendy had lied when she'd told me she'd tried the front door. She'd intended all along to slip in through the back, covertly, as a burglar would.

Her hostility toward Lucasta suddenly made sense to me, as did her lie about looking for extra blankets. I was convinced that she'd been searching for something much rarer and more valuable than an antique quilt or a puffy duvet. If the blanket chest's lid hadn't betrayed her, she would have carried on uninterrupted, safe in the knowledge that no one suspected her of anything duplicitous — no one but me and, to give credit where credit was due, Catchpole.

I didn't believe her story about staying in her room all day to work on her revised hiking route, either. She hadn't been holed up in her room. She'd been working her way from one end of Ladythorne to the other, hunting for hidden diamonds.

"I *knew* she was up to no good." I stomped my foot for added emphasis, spun around, and sprinted out of the library. As Catchpole had so wisely pointed out, cornered beasts could be dangerous. It would be foolish to confront one on my own. If I was going to keep Wendy from stuffing the Peacock parure into her backpack, I'd need Jamie's help.

A fluttery wash of golden light showed under Jamie's door, as if his fire had burned low while he slept. I felt a twinge of guilt at the thought of waking him, but tapped on his door nonetheless. I wasn't overly concerned about disturbing Wendy in her room across the hall because I was quite sure she wasn't there. I had no doubt whatsoever that she was at that moment prowling through the abbey with her pry bar and her head lamp, in search of the magnificent parure.

"Jamie," I said in an urgent whisper. "Jamie, are you up? Let me in."

I was about to knock more loudly when the door swung open and Jamie appeared, tousled and sleepy-eyed and clad in nothing but a pair of thermal long johns.

"Lori?" he asked. "What is it? Do you need blankets?"

"No," I told him. "I need you. May I come in?"

Jamie stood aside and I slipped into a room that was as masculine as mine was feminine. A pair of muscular bronze horses flanked the inlaid ebony clock on the oak mantelpiece, and the walls were covered in a stunning midnight-blue silk that shimmered in the fading firelight like the surface of a moonlit pool. The deeply carved four-poster bed was hung with blue-and-red tartan drapes that matched the rumpled duvet and complimented the red silk sheets. A tartan armchair and matching ottoman were grouped with a round, burled walnut table before the hearth, and the two tall windows opposite the door flanked a capacious roll-top desk and a revolving desk chair that might have come straight from Grundy DeClerke's Victorian business office.

Jamie's oil lamp, its wick turned low, sat on the roll-top desk, holding down one corner of a large, oblong sheet of paper. I was assailed by another twinge of guilt for waking him when I spied his jeans and dark-blue sweater in a heap at the foot of the bed. He'd clearly been too tired to fold them properly before he'd slid between those soft red sheets.

"Could you put your sweater on?" I asked, turning to face him. I wanted to focus on the matter at hand, and Jamie's naked torso silhouetted against the shimmering blue silk was ruining my concentration.

He rubbed his eyes with the heels of his hands, then cocked his head to one side. "You want me to put clothes on? Forgive me. I was under the impression that you wanted me to take them off."

"Wrong." I shook my head vehemently and stumbled back a step, then told myself not to be ungracious. "Not that it wouldn't be . . . That is, not that you're repellent or anything. To be perfectly honest, I find you incredibly not repellent, but be that as it may, when I said I needed you, I didn't mean it that way." I paused to catch my breath, then motioned to the pile of clothes. "Actually, it might be best if you put all of your clothes on. I've got sort of a long story to tell you and I'd feel terrible if you caught a cold while I was telling it."

Jamie had begun smiling midway through my stream of semi-coherent babble, evidently detecting in it something that vaguely resembled a compliment. When I stopped babbling, he simply nodded and moved toward his clothes.

While Jamie dressed, I applied myself to replenishing the fire and devising a way of giving him the facts without mentioning how I'd learned them. I'd already decided to substitute Bill for Aunt Dimity, and by the time Jamie had finished dressing, I was prepared to spill a carefully chosen selection of beans.

I perched on the ottoman and gestured for him to take the tartan armchair. He sat with his hands folded across his stomach, relaxed and attentive. If he was surprised at being dragged out of bed in the middle of the night by a wild-eyed woman, he didn't show it. Perhaps, I thought, it had happened to him so often that the novelty had worn thin.

"My husband phoned after I got back to my room," I began, keeping to my impromptu script. "It seems that when Tessa Gibbs purchased Ladythorne, she came into possession of a box full of Lucasta DeClerke's private papers. She sent the papers to Bill a couple of weeks ago, to see if they had any legal implications. He was going through them tonight and he discovered something extremely interesting. You remember the photo album you found in the library?"

Jamie listened without comment while I

hurriedly described the Peacock parure, the uproar over its alleged theft, and my suspicion — framed as Bill's — that the glorious set of jewelry had never been stolen and remained, contrary to Lucasta's claims, hidden somewhere in the abbey. It wasn't until I'd finished galloping through Wendy's scheme to avenge her father by purloining the parure that he spoke.

"You're making a great many assumptions, Lori."

"But it makes sense," I insisted.

"Does it?" Jamie got to his feet and walked to the roll-top desk. When he returned, he was holding the Jubilee album. "I took the album from the library. I found the photographs compelling and wanted to study them more closely." He sat in the armchair and handed the album to me. "And while I hate to point out the obvious, I have to say that *marksman* isn't an exclusively military term. Anyone who shoots can be a marksman. Perhaps Wendy's father is a hunter."

"So Wendy didn't take the album and we don't have a good reason to think that her father was a soldier." I folded my arms and said unhappily, "You're doing it again, Jamie."

"What am I doing?" he asked.

"You're being reasonable." I set the heavy album on the floor and eyed Jamie reproachfully. "You're talking me out of trusting my instincts."

"What if your instincts can't be trusted?" Jamie leaned forward, his elbows on his knees. "Tell me honestly: Do you like Wendy Walker?"

"Not much," I acknowledged. "She makes me feel stupid and helpless and soppy and she said some unkind things about Lucasta, but that's not what this is about, Jamie. I'm not letting personal prejudice affect my judgment. I honestly believe that Wendy came to Ladythorne in order to steal the Peacock parure."

"I know you do, Lori, but —"

"Okay," I broke in, waving him to silence. "I'll make a deal with you. We'll go to Wendy's room right now. If she's there, I'll admit that I was wrong about her. If she's not, you'll admit that I may be right."

I began to push myself up from the ottoman, but Jamie planted his palms on my shoulders and held me in place.

"No." His voice, like his touch, was gentle but firm. "I'm charmed by your company, Lori, but I doubt that Wendy will feel the same way. She deserves a good night's rest. We are not going to disturb her."

"But Jamie —"

"We'll speak with her in the morning," he proposed. "In the meantime, why don't you go back to your own bed?" His hands slid slowly down my arms and his eyes caught fire again. "Unless, of course, you've changed your mind about sharing mine."

"I haven't changed my mind about anything." I shook off his hands, stood, and stalked over to stare out the darkened window to the right of the roll-top desk. My disappointment was so great that I wasn't remotely tempted by the prospect of a night between those crimson sheets with a man I found incredibly not repellent. "If you won't help me hunt for Wendy, will you at least help me find the parure before she does? Two people can cover more ground than one."

Jamie's face, reflected in the darkened windowpanes, seemed to float disembodied through the air as he rose from the armchair and crossed to stand behind me.

"Of course I'll help you, Lori." He was so close that his warm breath ruffled my curls. "I'll help in any way I can. Shall we start right here, in my room? There's some beautiful, intricate carving on my headboard." He used a fingertip to draw a curlicue across the nape of my neck. "Let's see if we can open a hidden compartment."

I couldn't keep myself from trembling, and as disappointment eased, temptation beckoned. I cleared my throat and stepped resolutely, if a bit unsteadily, toward the desk. Jamie followed, and for a moment the urge to lean back into his arms, to tilt my head to one side and feel his soft beard against my neck, was so strong that I could scarcely breathe.

"You take the . . . the headboard," I managed, trying in vain to sound strong-willed and decisive. "I'll start with the, uh, desk. Lots . . . of . . . pigeonholes . . ."

My unfocused gaze came to rest on the oblong sheet of paper I'd noticed earlier. It appeared to be a floor plan, hand drawn on fine linen paper and labeled in an old-fashioned script that was strangely familiar. I leaned forward for a closer look, and felt goose flesh rise all up and down my arms. The small, precise handwriting was identical to the writing I'd seen on the labeled photo albums in the library.

" 'Ladythorne Abbey,' " I read aloud. " 'Service rooms.' "

"Lori?" Jamie's voice seemed to come from a long way away. "I can explain. . . ."

I straightened slowly as a thousand confused thoughts tumbled through my head, then swung around as the bedroom door opened.

Wendy Walker backed stealthily into the room, turning her head from side to side, as if making sure the corridor was empty. She was wearing her miner's lamp and carrying a brown-paper-wrapped parcel under one arm. After closing the door with great care, she turned the headlamp off, shifted the parcel to both hands, and said, "The floor plans are reliable, Jamie. Apart from the attics, nothing's been —" She broke off as she caught sight of me, shifted her gaze immediately to Jamie, and began to inch back toward the door. "Sorry. I didn't realize that you two were . . . I can see that you want to be alone, so I'll —"

"You're not going anywhere!" I cried.

I dodged Jamie's grasping hands and darted forward to grab at the parcel. Wendy jerked it away from me, lost her grip on it, and sent the parcel flying in an arc across the room. It tumbled end over end through the air, landed hard on the hearth rug, and burst open.

I gasped and time seemed to stand still as a waterfall of diamonds spilled across the dark blue rug to lie sparkling in the dancing firelight.

Fifteen

I don't know how long I stood there, openmouthed and staring, mesmerized by the glittering treasure that lay strewn across the rug. I felt as if I'd stumbled into Ali Baba's cave. There it was before me, the Peacock parure in all its glory — the delicate tiara, the exquisite bracelets, the teardrop earrings, the pair of brooches, the choker, the magnificent necklace — a king's ransom and more spread across the dark blue rug like a galaxy of stars flung carelessly across the midnight sky.

After what seemed an eternity something brushed my wrist and I realized that Jamie had reached out to me. I flinched as though scalded, snapped out of my reverie, and backed away from him until I bumped into the bed.

"*You* . . ." I exhaled the word in a whisper so venomous that he recoiled. My gaze traveled from the floor plan to the Jubilee album and back again to the parure, and I swayed, dizzied by the fathomless depths of my own stupidity. I'd known from the beginning that nothing but an extraordinary twist of fate would bring three Americans together in such a little-known and isolated place. I knew now that I was the only one of the three who'd come to Ladythorne by accident.

The truth lanced through my brain like bolts of lightning. It was Jamie's father who'd been the soldier, Jamie's father who'd been wounded, sent to the abbey, and cast out by a madwoman's lies. It was Jamie who'd come to Ladythorne to steal the parure, to avenge his father in the face of Lucasta's false accusations and the torment her vindictive letters had inflicted on him.

Jamie had seemed so sensitive, so protective, when he'd offered to cut short Catchpole's gloomy reminiscences during dinner. I realized now that the offer hadn't been an act of gallantry — my knight in shining armor had just been fishing for an excuse to shut the old man up before I learned too much about Lucasta.

Worse still, Jamie hadn't stopped by my door the night before simply to request the pleasure of my company. He'd wanted to make sure I was tucked away in my bedroom before he snuck off to the library, to hunt for clues that would lead him to the parure's hiding place. By the time I'd burst in on him, he'd already discovered the Jubilee album, and I'd shown him where to find the floor plans.

Jamie had directed Wendy's search. He'd masterminded their scheme, sending her to do the legwork while he plotted their next maneuver. He'd instructed her to meet him in the library. She hadn't whispered his name through the barricaded door by chance, but because she'd expected to find *him* there, not me. His concern for my well-being, his interest in books, his delightful conversation had been nothing but a smokescreen raised to keep me from seeing what was really going on.

I couldn't believe that I'd been so blind. The truth had been laid out before me as clearly as a wiring diagram, but I'd been too distracted by Jamie's charm to see it.

"Was that your job?" I asked him, tears of humiliation pricking my eyes. "Is that why you spent so much time with me today? Were you supposed to keep me *busy* while Wendy ransacked the abbey? Is that why you've been so *nice* to me?"

Jamie dropped his gaze.

"He didn't want to do it," Wendy put in, "anymore than I wanted to be rude to you. But we had to think of a way to —"

"Why?" I rounded on her. "Why would you have to think of anything when I was so incredibly cooperative? Jamie was the perfect baby-sitter. He took me in completely. If I wasn't with him, I was off at Catchpole's or up in my room." I swiped angrily at a tear that had trickled down my cheek. "I gave you buckets of time to poke around the house with that pry bar of yours, Wendy. I gave you more time than you needed to steal the diamonds. *I found the bloody floor plans for you.* Aren't you going to thank me?"

"Lori . . ." Wendy said gently as she started to approach me.

"Don't you come near me," I snapped, stiffening. "My husband knows I'm here and he knows what I think of you. If anything happens to me, he'll come down on you like the wrath of God."

Wendy stopped dead in her tracks, stared at me for a moment, then flung her hands into the air.

"Oh, for pity's sake," she said. "I can't deal with this drama queen, Jamie. *You* try talking sense to her." She whipped off the head lamp, tossed it on the bed, and strode over to open the doors of Jamie's wardrobe.

I gaped at her in disbelief. "You're disgruntled? You take complete advantage of me, and *you're* disgruntled?"

"I'm not disgruntled, I'm hungry," Wendy replied, reaching into the wardrobe. "Lunch was ages ago, and I haven't spent the evening sitting around and talking. I've worked up an appetite."

I was about to ask how she could think of food at a time like this when my stomach betrayed me with a highly audible rumble. I blushed, then watched, nonplussed, as Wendy slid a silver tray from a shelf in the wardrobe and carried it to the walnut table.

The tray held two sets of silverware, a pair of tumblers, a large bottle of mineral water, and an assortment of tins, jars, and packets containing an array of expensive nibbles: beluga caviar, pâté de foie gras, herring fillets in mustard sauce, rolled anchovies with capers, smoked mussels, smoked baby clams, olives, gherkins, pickled pearl onions, cream crackers, cheesy biscuits, crunchy breadsticks — it was all I could do to keep from drooling as Wendy passed by.

"Don't forget the bowl," said Jamie. He retrieved a covered stoneware bowl from the wardrobe and set it on the hearth, close to the fire. "It's Catchpole's apricot compote. It should be warmed through by the time we finish the main course."

While Wendy slid the ottoman to the opposite side of the table from the armchair and filled the tumblers with water, Jamie rummaged through his backpack until he found a small plastic cup and a set of camping cutlery, which he used to create a third place setting. He then moved the desk chair to the walnut table and swiveled it to face me.

"Please, Lori," he said. "Won't you join us?"

I was overcome by a sense of unreality. What kind of crooks were they? I was an eyewitness to their crime. I'd caught them red-handed. They knew that my husband was a *lawyer,* for heaven's sake. Why were they offering me a midnight snack? The fact that no one had bothered to scoop up the diamonds or threaten me with grievous bodily harm was oddly reassuring, as was the curious tableau of tins and biscuits set against a backdrop of fabulous jewels, but still, I hesitated.

"Look, Lori." Wendy sat on the ottoman and pointed ostentatiously at the silver tray. "The packets are sealed. You're safe. No poison."

"Wendy," Jamie said repressively. He placed a hand on the back of the chair. "Please join us, Lori. Please give me a chance to apologize . . . and to explain."

It wasn't Jamie's attitude of humble penitence or his evident desire to make a clean breast of things that ultimately persuaded me to accept his invitation. My stomach cast the deciding vote with a growl so filled with yearning that I was forced to take pity on it.

I swiveled the chair to face the table, sat, and stared straight at the fire, refusing to make eye contact with either of the co-conspirators.

"Thank you." Jamie lowered himself into the tartan armchair and began opening tins.

"Catchpole will kill you when he finds out you've raided the pantry," I muttered.

"I didn't hear you complain at lunch." Wendy reached for the cheesy biscuits. "I seem to recall three bowls of paella disappearing into your gullet."

I'd intended to maintain an aloof silence during the meal, as a sign of my disapproval and a tribute to my grievously wounded pride, but as Emma Harris had reminded me not so very long ago, I wasn't any good at maintaining silence, aloof or otherwise. I quickly decided that a few scathing comments would serve the same purpose with less strain.

"Now I know why you had no appetite yesterday," I said. "At the time I thought you were afraid of Lucasta's ghost, but of course, I know better now. You weren't afraid of the ghost. You were afraid Catchpole might get in your way, might even keep you from stealing the parure." I slathered a cream cracker with a generous helping of pâté. "No wonder you couldn't clean your plates."

Wendy's gray eyes narrowed ominously. She opened her mouth to speak, but Jamie intervened, holding his arms out as if to separate two overzealous sparring partners.

"Let's eat first, then talk," he pleaded. "It's impossible to think clearly on an empty stomach."

Conversation ceased. My scathing comment had inadvertently enabled me to achieve my original goal of silence, but it didn't last long. Many hours had passed since we'd eaten the paella, and the coconut ginger soup had been more of a snack than a meal, so our appetites were sharp. We vacuumed up every tasty morsel on the tray in record time and attacked the apricot compote like a trio of hyenas.

Wendy had already placed the ravished tray and the empty stoneware bowl on the floor in the corridor and returned to the ottoman when the ebony clock began to chime midnight. When the last echoing note had faded, Jamie leaned forward, his elbows on his knees, his fingers loosely interlaced.

"God knows, you have every right to be furious with me, Lori," he said. "I'm furious with myself for . . . misleading you. If it's any consolation, it wasn't mere playacting. I meant what I said in the library. I've enjoyed every moment of our time together. I like you very much."

I gave a derisive snort. "If this is how you treat people you like, I'd hate to see how you treat those you dislike."

"You've seen one short phrase in an epic tale," said Jamie. "I'll tell you the rest, if you'll let me. You have no reason to believe a word I say, but I hope you'll listen. I hope you'll reserve your final judgment until after you've heard me out."

Jamie had, unknowingly, hit upon the one strategy against which I had no defenses. I'd never been able to resist the lure of storytelling. My childhood had been filled with the sound of my mother's voice recounting Aunt Dimity's adventures, and

I'd devoted a good chunk of my adult life to working with books. I had no doubt that Jamie was about to produce a work of fiction, but I wasn't going anywhere, and I was curious to see how he'd twist and turn the plot to make himself the hero.

I folded my arms and said testily, "Go ahead. I'm listening."

He leaned back in the chair and gazed into the fire with a concentrated frown, as if trying to recall a complicated series of events.

"Imagine if you will," he began, "two American soldiers. We'll call them James and Walter."

"Wally," Wendy said stiffly. "Everyone called him Wally."

I gave her a sharp glance and knew with a sudden certainty that she was speaking of her father. A moment's reflection told me, with equal certainty, that Jamie had been named for James, his father. I looked from Wendy's somber face to Jamie's and felt for the first time that I was a stranger intruding on a shared and private grief. I wondered uncomfortably what it must be costing them to confide in me.

"We'll call him Wally, then." Jamie nodded gravely, then went on. "James, the older of the two, was a captain. Wally was his driver. James and Wally had fought side by side for three years. They'd spent D-day, like your father, storming Omaha Beach. They'd pushed through the Battle of the Bulge and nearly reached the outskirts of Berlin when a sniper stopped them."

"They were very young when they were shot," Wendy added, as though reminding Jamie of a significant detail. "James was only twenty-three and Wally had just turned twenty."

"Wally was nearly twenty years younger than I am now," Jamie said. He meditated in silence, then seemed to reach a decision. He stood. "Shall we take a walk? I find that a stroll after a meal aids digestion. Apart from that, there are a few things I'd like to show you, Lori, to illustrate the story, so to speak."

I went along with his odd request, rising from the desk chair and motioning for him to lead the way. The meal and Jamie's calm demeanor had soothed my much-abused nerves. I wasn't sure where we were going, but I was no longer afraid that my companions would beat me to death with the pry bar and dump my body in the blanket chest.

Before we left the room, Wendy knelt to

gather the jewels. She bundled them into the brown paper wrapping and tucked the parcel beneath a pile of blankets atop Jamie's wardrobe.

"In case Catchpole decides to do a bed check," she explained, and retrieved Jamie's oil lamp from the desk.

We walked three abreast down the corridor, Wendy lighting the way with the oil lamp while Jamie spoke in a low-voiced murmur, as though unwilling to disturb the slumbering house.

"After James and Wally were wounded, they were evacuated to England. The medicos didn't think they were strong enough to endure a transatlantic crossing, so the two friends were sent to a convalescent home in England, a place buried deep in the countryside, where no German bombs had fallen. A place called Ladythorne Abbey."

He fell silent as we descended the main staircase and didn't speak again until we'd reached the entrance hall.

"They'd never seen anything like it." His deep voice echoed in the cavernous space. He extended a hand to one of the rosewood angels capping the newel posts, traced the graceful curve of a wing with a fingertip, then stepped toward the center of the hall and let his gaze wander from the beaten copper bowl on the console table to the armorial medallions dotting the coffered ceiling. "The great country houses they'd seen in France and Germany had been badly damaged during the war, but Ladythorne, hidden in its secret valley, was untouched, remote, romantic."

He turned abruptly, took the oil lamp from Wendy, and crossed to a set of imposing double doors set in the wall to the right of the staircase. He pushed the doors open and stood to one side, motioning with his head for me to precede him. I hesitated, then stepped past him into a room that dwarfed the entrance hall, both in size and grandeur. Jamie followed on my heels and held the lamp high, but the increased illumination only made the room seem more fantastic.

Great darkened oak beams ribbed the white-plastered ceiling, each hung with a black wrought-iron wagon-wheel chandelier. A cavernous stone fireplace dominated the far wall, with a raised and painted coat of arms set into an elaborate oak overmantel crowned with fluted pinnacles that reached almost to the ceiling. An enormous Axminster carpet woven in rich blues and reds and golds ran the length of the room, anchoring islands of chintz-covered armchairs, hobnailed leather sofas, and tables that held silver-framed photographs, leather-bound books, bowls of fragrant potpourri, and a collection of small bronzes.

The outer wall was pierced by a dozen slender stained-glass windows resplendent with Gothic tracery, but my eyes turned toward the inner wall, which was nearly covered by three multicolored tapestries. In one, a falcon flew from the gloved fist of its handler; in another, a pack of hounds bayed at a treed fox while a pair of mounted huntsmen looked on. In the third, an archer drew his bow and aimed his arrow at a fleeing flock of doves. Although the colors had been dimmed and the needlework had worn in places over time, the images retained a sense of life and movement that took my breath away.

Behind me, Jamie murmured, "If the Great Hall's rendered you speechless, Lori, imagine its effect on two weak and wide-eyed young men who'd spent three years in hell."

Sixteen

"The Great Hall didn't look like this when they first saw it, of course." Jamie walked toward the yawning fireplace at the far end of the room, gesturing as he went, as if to draw a picture in the air. "When James and Wally arrived at Ladythorne, the Great Hall was furnished with rows of hospital beds, with IV bottles on wheeled poles, with curtained frames that could be moved to shield a failing patient from prying eyes. It didn't smell of potpourri, but of disinfectant and fear. Even so" — Jamie paused to gaze up at the plastered ceiling — "the oak beams were still in place, and the stained glass. And the men didn't spend all of their time here. Wonder of wonders, they were allowed to roam freely throughout the house."

He stopped, turned on his heel, and made for a door to my right, between the two nearest tapestries. Wendy and I hastened after him into a spacious oak-paneled room furnished with a carved and gilded billiards table, racks of inlaid cues and ivory balls, small tables set with cut-glass glasses and decanters, and an assortment of leather-covered chairs.

I ran my hand over the intricately carved phoenix whose widespread wings covered one end of the billiards table and experienced a strange sense of displacement, as if we'd shifted back in time to the years when Ladythorne had been a refuge from the storm of war. I could almost see the ghostly silhouettes of convalescent soldiers, some on crutches, bending over their cues, while others with their arms in slings sprawled lazily in the leather chairs, calling words of advice or ridicule to the players.

Jamie didn't pause for commentary, but moved through the billiards room to the smoking room beyond. The humidors, bamboo newspaper racks, and ample armchairs gave the smoking room the relaxed and intimate air of a traditional gentlemen's club. I suspected that the quieter soldiers had found their way here, the ones who preferred solitary reflection to billiards-room banter.

Jamie must have studied the floor plans minutely because he moved unerringly to a door concealed in the smoking room's dark paneling. He silently beckoned to us to follow, and led the way through a short passage that delivered us to a place so magical I couldn't quite believe my eyes. To a man who'd spent three years in combat, it would have looked like a preview of heaven.

A conservatory had been grafted onto the back of the house. Slender ribs of white-painted iron fanned out from a conical roof to connect in delicate loops with the glass walls' lacy ironwork. Three-tiered slatted wooden shelves lined the walls, supported on wrought-iron legs that mimicked twining vines festooned with rosebuds. The floor wore a gleaming mosaic of spring blossoms, and the dainty wrought-iron table and chairs seemed cry out for teacups and lace-adorned ladies with parasols.

The conservatory would have been sweetly pretty, surrounded and filled by the soft greens of summer, but the blizzard had transformed it into a palace fit for an ice queen. The conical roof wore a towering crown of snow, fat flakes swirled and drifted in the darkness beyond, and every shimmering pane of glass was rimed with glittering feathers and flames and forests of frost. The air was so cold that I could see my breath, but I would have stood there until I, too, was covered in frost, if Jamie hadn't taken my arm and guided me back into the house.

"We'll return to my room," he said. "You've seen enough, for now."

Jamie's lamp was running low on oil, so I fetched mine from my room before returning to his. I placed the lamp on the walnut table, pulled the duvet from the bed and wrapped it around me, then curled up in the tartan armchair while Jamie worked on building up the fire.

When he'd finished, he settled in the desk chair, but Wendy chose to sit cross-legged on the floor, with her back against the ottoman, holding her hands out to the flames. After our sojourn through Ladythorne's frigid corridors, even a rugged outdoorswoman like Wendy welcomed the chance to savor the fire's warmth.

I needed the quiet moment to come back to earth. I knew myself well enough to realize that I was in danger of being swept off my feet by Ladythorne's loveliness. I couldn't allow myself to be distracted by its charms anymore than I could permit myself to fall prey once again to Jamie's. I reminded myself sternly that I already knew the end of the story, and that however Jamie chose to justify his actions, a crime was still a crime.

The ebony clock chimed the quarter hour. Forty-five minutes had passed since we'd left the bedroom.

"I'm sure you've guessed the purpose of our tour, Lori," Jamie said. "I wanted you to see what James and Wally saw. I wanted you to walk in their footsteps. Those two war-weary young men must have felt as if Ladythorne had been plucked from an Arthurian legend, with its bell tower, its cloister, and its pretty chatelaine."

Wendy turned her head to look directly at me. "No one told James or Wally about Lucasta's fiancé," she stated firmly. "They didn't know he'd died at Dunkirk, and they didn't know that her father had been killed in the Blitz. Lucasta must have ordered the servants and staff not to mention her personal tragedies. If James and Wally had known . . ." She faltered, turned back to the fire, and fell silent.

"But they didn't know," Jamie reiterated. "As far as they could tell, Lucasta DeClerke was a vastly wealthy young heiress with a charitable streak, who hadn't a care in the world."

I nodded as Dimity's words came back to me: *I found her almost too bright, too cheerful. Everyone spoke of how brave she was, but I couldn't help wondering if she was concealing a great deal of anger behind her pretty smile. I couldn't be sure, of course. People sometimes are what they present themselves to be. . . .* If Dimity, knowing of Lucasta's losses, had been unable to see through the girl's cheerful facade, what chance had James and Wally had?

"I think I understand what you're getting at," I said. "James and Wally were a pair of humble GIs who saw Lucasta DeClerke as a fairy princess living in a castle. The poor guys must have been shocked and disappointed when the princess turned into an ogre, but that still doesn't give you the right to —"

Wendy sniffed impatiently. "If jumping to conclusions were an Olympic sport, you'd have a closet filled with gold medals," she scolded. "Will you please try for one minute to pretend that you don't know everything?"

I wanted to fire back a snappy retort, but since I'd already jumped to an embarrassingly large number of wrong conclusions, I couldn't argue Wendy's point.

"Sorry," I said stiffly, and told Jamie to go on.

"The next part of the story isn't as clear as the rest," he said, "but I think I can guess what happened. As James and Wally regained their strength, they began to explore the abbey."

"Wally was interested in architecture," Wendy put in, "so he spent time studying the structure of the house and the outbuildings surrounding it. He would have loved the conservatory."

"He would have feasted on Ladythorne like a starving man at a banqueting table," Jamie said with a wan smile. "James, who'd always been bookish, explored Ladythorne's library, where he happened upon an album filled with fascinating photographs."

He bent to lift the Jubilee album from the floor, placed it on the walnut table, and paged through it until he came to the photograph of Grundy and Rose DeClerke, costumed as Night and Day. Their faces seemed strangely alive in the quivering firelight.

"One photograph in particular fired his imagination," Jamie murmured, gazing down at the fabulous image. "When asked, the servants told him that the jewels were real and that Miss DeClerke had them in her possession, but that she'd hidden them so cunningly that she alone knew where to find them."

"Wally must have found the floor plans by then." Wendy jerked her chin toward the roll-top desk. "Jamie tells me they were in the library, so I suppose James could have found them. Or maybe Lucasta loaned the plans to Wally, to help him learn more about the house. Whatever the case, the two friends put the floor plans together with the tale of the Peacock parure and decided to go on a treasure hunt. It may seem frivolous, but —" She broke off when I shook my head.

I had no trouble understanding the treasure hunt's appeal. James and Wally had been little more than kids. They'd been transported from hell to a magical place untouched by enemy bombs. How could they resist the excitement of a treasure hunt? How could they resist anything that would allow them to forget, if only for a while, the carnage of Omaha Beach?

"It doesn't seem frivolous at all," I said. "Did you come here to finish the hunt for them?"

"We didn't have to," Wendy replied, "because they succeeded. They were determined young men with time on their hands. They found the parure."

I looked in confusion from her face to Jamie's. He ran the tip of his tongue over his lips, as if his mouth had gone dry, and when he spoke, he seemed to be speaking to the mustachioed man and the sturdy, round-faced woman gazing serenely back at him from the Jubilee album.

"I don't think they intended to steal the jewels," he said, "but when they saw the diamonds shining like a thousand suns, they . . . they couldn't help themselves. Surely you can understand what drove them to it. Lucasta was a wealthy young woman destined to one day marry an equally wealthy man. She'd never have to worry about earning a living or paying a mortgage or feeding a growing family. The parure could make no possible difference in her life, but it would make a world of difference in theirs. It would make all of their dreams come —"

"Hold on," I broke in, my thoughts in disarray. "What are you saying, Jamie? Are you telling me that —"

Jamie's dark eyes locked on mine. "I'm telling you that Wendy and I aren't trying to steal the parure. We're trying to put it back."

Seventeen

My head spun as the last of my preconceptions struggled frantically to realign themselves. If I'd understood Jamie correctly, he'd just accused his own father, and Wendy's, of committing a despicable act against a young woman who'd treated them with nothing but kindness. If Jamie was telling the truth, then I'd been wrong, Dimity had been wrong, and — most important of all — the military authorities had been wrong to ignore Lucasta's cries for help.

"Let me get this straight," I managed. "Are you saying that the theft *actually happened?* Are you telling me that James and Wally *stole* the Peacock parure?"

Jamie nodded, once. He closed the Jubilee album, but remained sitting forward in his chair, his head bowed, his long hair curtaining his face. "Captain James Macrae was my father. Corporal Walter Walker was Wendy's father. Captain Macrae and Corporal Walker stole the parure, divided it between them, and smuggled it out of England when they were shipped back to the States."

For one wrenching moment the only thing I could think about was Lucasta, railing against the men who'd betrayed her, demanding justice, and receiving none.

"James and Wally lied to their commanding officers." Jamie's voice was barely audible. "They lied to the men with whom they'd served. When others were accused of the theft, they said nothing. They hurt an innocent girl who'd already been hurt beyond comprehension. I believe their actions drove her mad." He pinched the bridge of his nose wearily. "I wish you'd been right, Lori. I wish I were a clever criminal, but I'm not. All I'm trying to do is to make amends for my father's sins."

"And my father's," Wendy said bitterly. She drew her knees to her chest and wrapped her arms around them. "Let's not forget that half the blame lies with Wally. He would've taken the secret with him to the grave if Jamie's father hadn't shocked him into speaking."

I heard the complex emotions in her voice, the deep love and the disillusion, and felt a pang of envy. I'd never known my father well enough to feel much of anything for him. He'd died before I'd learned to talk.

My mother had been the hero of my life, and though she'd kept her share of secrets from me, she'd never committed any sin for which I had to atone. I couldn't put myself in my companions' shoes, but I could recognize heartache when I saw it. I had no doubt that they were telling the truth, a truth they both found difficult to bear. Captain Macrae and Corporal Walker hadn't broken faith with Lucasta alone when they'd stolen the parure. In the end, they'd betrayed their children's trust as well.

I felt a sudden impulse to rise quietly, return to my room, and leave Jamie and Wendy to complete their private act of expiation in peace, but before I could move, Wendy went on with the story. She spoke with her face turned toward the fire and continued to refer to her father by his first name, as though to distance herself from his misdeeds.

"Wally never talked about the war," she said. "I knew by the scars on his chest that he'd been wounded, but he never told me what happened. He never attended a single reunion of his old army buddies. He never told me about his good friend James."

Jamie confirmed that his father had been similarly reticent.

"Then how did you find out about the parure?" I asked.

"In my case, it started with the Alzheimer's." Jamie leaned back in his chair, his hands resting lightly on the arms. "When the disease took hold of my father, he became obsessed with memories of the war. His disjointed recollections didn't make much sense to me, but I listened because . . . because he was my father." Jamie took a shaky breath and let it out slowly. "It wasn't easy. He kept apologizing for hurting a girl he'd met in England, a Lady Thorne. He said he hadn't known about her sweetheart and her dad. I thought he was talking about a wartime fling, so I didn't mention his ramblings to my mother. I didn't realize that he was making a last-ditch effort to confess to something far more serious. Then Wendy called."

Wendy had spent the previous Fourth of July weekend with her parents at their home in Long Island. On the morning of the Fourth, the telephone had rung. Her father had answered it and been struck down by a massive stroke.

"I found him lying on the floor, muttering about his faults," she said. "He gripped my arm and whispered: 'Put it back.' I thought he was talking about the telephone, but before I could put it back on the hook, he died."

Wendy blamed the phone call for her father's death. When she traced the call, she learned that it had come from a VA hospital in Illinois. After the funeral, she telephoned the hospital. Jamie answered. She'd reached his father's room.

"I didn't believe Wendy, at first," Jamie admitted. "I thought Father was too far gone to use the telephone, but when she mentioned Wally's name, I began to pay attention. A soldier named Wally had cropped up often in Father's ramblings. 'Put it back, Wally,' he'd say. 'We have to put it back.' "

"The same words Wally breathed in my ear as he lay dying." Wendy drew her arms more tightly around her knees. "Two old soldiers, saying the same words — it had to mean something. Had they known each other? What did they need to put back? Did it have something to do with this woman, this Lady Thorne?"

"We needed answers," said Jamie. "To find them, we dug into the past."

Army records revealed that James and Wally had served and been wounded together, and that Ladythorne wasn't a woman, but a convalescent home in England. Further research led Wendy to eleven other American officers who'd been at the abbey near the end of the war in Europe. The eleven men remembered James and Wally, and gave vivid accounts of Ladythorne's beauty and comfort, but said nothing about the scandal that had erupted during their stay there.

"That's when I found the letters," Jamie continued. "Father kept his army gear in a trunk in the attic. I was going through the trunk one day when I noticed a loose floorboard underneath it. Father had hidden two ammunition boxes in the cavity below the loose floorboard. The boxes held hundreds of letters. They were hateful, spiteful things, signed by a woman named Lucasta DeClerke." Jamie rested his head against the back of the chair and gazed toward the ceiling. "I don't think Father knew about Lucasta's father and her fiancé until he read her letters, and even then he couldn't have known how they died. She didn't include the details."

"We didn't know until Catchpole told us during lunch yesterday," Wendy interjected. "Hearing that her fiancé had been a soldier, that he'd died at Dunkirk, and that her father had been killed in a bombing raid — that's what spoiled my appetite."

"Mine as well." Jamie's brow furrowed. "I'm sure Father wouldn't have stolen the parure if he'd been aware of the sacrifices Lucasta had already made."

A faint note of uncertainty undermined Jamie's statement and told me that he wasn't sure of anything anymore. Would his father have behaved differently if he'd understood the full extent of Lucasta's suffering? Jamie would never know. I recalled the stillness that had come over him when Catchpole had mentioned Lucasta's ghost. Perhaps, I thought, Jamie sensed her restless spirit in the house. Perhaps he felt as though he deserved to be haunted.

"Lucasta had written to Wally, too," said Wendy. "It wasn't until Jamie described James's letters that I remembered the ones Wally had gotten. They were identical to the ones under the floorboard — ivory envelopes, handwritten addresses, foreign stamps. Wally tossed them, unopened, into our wood stove as soon as they arrived."

"Father kept every one," Jamie said. "They helped me understand what he was trying to say to me. I realized as I read them that he'd been struggling desperately to tell me that he and Wally had stolen the parure."

"Wally couldn't burn Lucasta's letters fast enough." Wendy unfolded her legs, seized the poker, and stabbed savagely at the fire. "He was too cowardly to face the truth, and he didn't want me to know about it, ever."

What father would? I wondered. No father would want his daughter to know about the mistakes he'd made, especially if she worshipped him as unreservedly as, I suspected, Wendy had worshipped her father. I felt a rush of sympathy for Wally. How could he confide in a daughter who would judge him so severely? How could he risk the hard fall from the high pedestal on which she'd placed him?

Wendy slumped back against the ottoman, her flash of temper spent. "We found out that Lucasta had written to each of them, each of the Americans who'd been at Ladythorne when the robbery occurred. Most of the men thought she was batty, but a few weren't so sure."

The military's refusal to investigate the theft had driven Lucasta to take matters into her own hands. She'd spent the rest of her life writing to the men she suspected of stealing the parure. She cursed the thieves.

She assured them they'd never profit from their crime. She berated and belittled and badgered them so persistently that she managed to arouse an element of suspicion in three of the accused. Those three kept a watchful eye on the rest.

"Lucasta's curse worked," Wendy commented succinctly. "Neither Wally nor James ever profited from their crime. They couldn't sell the jewels because they were being watched too closely. If their bank accounts got too fat too fast, vague suspicions might have hardened into accusations."

Jamie shifted uneasily in his chair. "There was something else that prevented Father from selling the jewels: My mother had been a nurse during the war. She would never have forgiven him for robbing a woman who'd dedicated herself so selflessly to helping the wounded. When she accepted Father's long-distance proposal of marriage, he put the necklace and the earrings into a canteen pouch, hid the pouch under another floorboard in the attic, and tried to forget about it."

"Wally stashed the tiara, the brooches, and the bracelets in a coffee can under his workbench," Wendy added. "It took me a month to find them."

"Why didn't they send them back?" I asked. "Once James and Wally realized they couldn't sell the jewels, why didn't they mail them back to Lucasta, anonymously?"

Wendy's eyebrows rose. "You've seen the parure, Lori. Would you trust it to the postal system?"

"I suppose not," I conceded.

"They could have brought the parure back in person," Wendy observed, "if they'd been willing to own up to what they'd done, if they'd had the courage to face the consequences."

"They wouldn't have faced the consequences alone." Jamie sounded tired and a tiny bit impatient, as if he'd made the same point many times before. "Can you imagine how loudly Lucasta would have crowed if she'd been proven right after all these years? She wouldn't have agreed to settle things privately, Wendy. She would have dragged the army into it, and our families. The tabloids would have had a field day. Can't you see the headlines? YANKS PINCH FAMILY JEWELS — ARMY COVERS UP. Would you have wanted your mother to go through that kind of humiliation?"

"No," Wendy murmured, chastened.

"That's why I'm here."

Jamie got to his feet and paced restlessly to the darkened window. He stood facing it for a time, then turned, leaned back against the sill, and folded his arms.

"I would have found a way to return the jewels to Lucasta," he said, "but she was dead by the time I pieced together Father's story, and she left no heirs."

"So we decided to do what our fathers couldn't bring themselves to do," said Wendy. "Put it back."

It wasn't hard to fill in what happened next, but Jamie spelled it out for me. By making discreet inquiries among his Oxford friends he'd learned that Ladythorne Abbey would be deserted in February. He and Wendy had flown to England separately, with the jewels tucked into their backpacks, for all intents and purposes two innocent hikers anticipating the tranquility of winter's uncrowded trails. They'd planned to rendezvous at Ladythorne, enter the house surreptitiously, return the parure, and leave.

"Unfortunately, no one mentioned Catchpole," said Jamie. "And no one could have told us that a blizzard would send you our way."

"You were a mixed blessing, Lori."

Wendy tilted her head to one side. "On the one hand, you managed to tame Catchpole by threatening to sic your husband on him, for which we were grateful."

"On the other hand," Jamie continued, "you were far too bright not to notice that something odd was going on." He glanced at Wendy. "Especially when certain people ran around making loud noises in the dead of night."

"Stupid blanket chest," Wendy muttered. "How was I to know that the hinges were shot?"

Jamie turned back to me. "Apart from that, your husband had told you too much about Lucasta for our peace of mind. We had to think of a way to keep you from interfering with our task."

Wendy grinned mischievously. "Jamie agreed — reluctantly — to bat his big brown eyes at you. And I decided to be Miss Rude. I hoped you'd stomp off to your room in a snit after our little chat in the library last night, but you refused to budge. You wanted another glimpse of those brown eyes, right?"

"They're lovely eyes," I admitted, with a wry smile.

"They're beautiful," Wendy agreed, and flung her arm dramatically into the air.

"They're the kind of eyes that could make any woman —"

"All right, you two, that's enough." Jamie blushed to his roots. "I'm more sorry than I can say for my part in the deception, Lori. It's not something I . . . that is to say, I don't make a habit of . . ."

"It's okay, Jamie," I broke in, taking pity on him. "I'm a big girl. I'll get over it. So what's next? Can't you dump the parure in a drawer and be done with it?"

"I'm afraid it's not quite so simple." Jamie returned to the armchair. "In one of his last lucid moments, Father made me promise to put the parure back in its original hiding place."

"Which is . . . where?" I looked at him expectantly.

He and Wendy exchanged meaningful glances.

"We're not sure," he said finally. "The only hint Father gave — and he used hand gestures more than words — was that he and Wally found the parure in some sort of custom-fitted marble box."

"It's not in the attic storeroom," Wendy declared. "I went through every shelf up there it with a fine-tooth comb last night."

I gaped at her. "So Catchpole *wasn't* lying. He *did* see a light in the attics."

"I was up there when he left the abbey," said Wendy. "I suppose he could have seen the skylights flickering if he'd looked over his shoulder on the way to his cottage."

"He's used to seeing Ladythorne look a certain way," Jamie added. "Any change would stand out, even in a blizzard."

I gave Jamie a sour glance. "Your brain must have been working overtime to come up with all of those reasons why he couldn't have seen a light."

"Sorry," said Jamie.

I chuckled in spite of myself. "I have to hand it to you, you're quick on your feet. You didn't blink an eye when I opened the map case, even though you must have wanted to cheer at the sight of those floor plans."

"I may have looked calm," said Jamie, "but my heart was racing."

So was mine, I thought, and quickly looked down at my hands.

"The parure's special box isn't in the attic storeroom," Wendy repeated. "So that leaves us with two fairly sizable floors stuffed to the rafters with . . . stuff."

"Good grief," I muttered.

"Never fear," said Wendy. "The night is young, though not as young as it was." She looked up at the ticking clock. "We've wasted half of it in here, talking to you."

"Not wasted, I think." Jamie turned those wine-dark eyes toward me. "Three people can cover more ground than two. What do you say, Lori? Will you help us?"

I looked into his eyes and saw that he was asking not only for himself and for Wendy, but for those two war-weary soldiers whose treasure hunt had blighted Lucasta's life and riddled their own lives with regret and guilt. The secret they'd shared had divided them from the men who'd fought beside them on the battlefield. Worse, it had cut them off from each other. James never spoke of Wally. Wally never mentioned James. Each man had lost the best friend he'd ever had. Captain Macrae and Corporal Walker had paid a high price for the sins of their youth. If I could, in some small way, help their troubled souls to rest more peacefully, I would.

"Will I help?" I reached out to grip Jamie's hand. "Try stopping me."

Eighteen

We moved the lamps to the mantel shelf and spread the floor plans over the walnut table. Wendy explained that she'd spent the day carrying out a general reconnaissance of the house. By comparing her observations to the floor plans, Jamie had been able to confirm that, apart from the attics, Tessa Gibbs had made no radical alterations to the abbey's structure. Ladythorne's main floors were essentially the same as they had been when James and Wally had roamed its corridors.

I felt a bit discouraged when I realized that my theory regarding hidey-holes in the fabric of the house was no longer valid. Tessa Gibbs would have told Bill if her workmen had discovered a fortune's worth of jewels beneath a floorboard or behind a false wall, but she'd have no compelling reason to mention the discovery of an empty box. The same held true for my theory regarding shabby versus refinished furniture. An empty box found hidden in a rickety Queen Anne bureau might arouse mild curiosity, but it wasn't the sort of thing one discussed with one's lawyer.

"I don't think we should be too bothered by the changes Tessa Gibbs made in the attics," said Jamie. "According to the floor plans, they used to house the servants' quarters, and I doubt that a pair of GIs would be able to intrude on the servants without causing the kind of gossip that would bring them up before a disciplinary board."

"I can't believe I'm saying this," said Wendy, "but three cheers for the blizzard. It wasn't part of the plan, but it's given us the perfect excuse for staying put. If the weather gods are kind, the snow'll stick around until the end of the week and give us that much longer to hunt for the box."

"Where should we start?" I asked, bending over the walnut table.

"Pick a room, any room." Jamie raised his hands, palms upward. "The box could be hidden anywhere."

"I'm betting on the bell tower." Wendy tapped the plans decisively. "It's like an eagle's nest up there, with a circular view that overlooks the entire valley. If I'd been in Lucasta's shoes, I'd have spent a lot of time in the tower, brooding over the empty box and keeping an eye out for an American invasion."

I volunteered to search the second-story bedrooms. According to the plans, they'd originally been parceled out among Grundy DeClerke's four sons, but I was sure that one of the boys' rooms had been turned into a girl's room when Lucasta was born.

"Catchpole told us that Lucasta spent a lot of time in her room, after her mind began to go," I reminded them. "My guess is that she retreated to the room she'd had as a child, and took the box with her. She'd feel safe there, and she'd know every nook and cranny like the back of her hand."

"At least we won't have to worry about Catchpole raining on our parade," said Wendy. "He seems determined to stay in his cottage until we leave."

I ducked my head self-consciously and said, in a very small voice, "He might change his mind."

"Why should he?" Jamie peered at me closely. "Lori? What have you done?"

"I sort of . . . invited him to join us," I confessed. "I felt sorry for him. And I didn't know what you two were doing."

"Just what we need," muttered Wendy. "A cruise director."

"In that case," said Jamie, "I'd better work on the ground floor."

"To keep Catchpole from surprising us?" I said.

Jamie nodded. "If he shows his pretty face tomorrow, I'll convince him that you two frail beauties are spending the day confined to your beds."

"I'm not going to miss breakfast," Wendy grumbled mutinously.

"I'll bring it up to you on a tray," Jamie offered. He stroked his beard for a moment, then snapped his fingers. "Better yet, if Catchpole shows up, I'll have him bring breakfast to both of you. That way he'll be able to see for himself how weak and feeble you are."

I was, in fact, beginning to feel authentically weak and feeble. As the ebony clock chimed twice, the weight of the past two days closed in on me. In the past forty-eight hours, I'd fought my way through a raging blizzard, faced down a gun-toting lunatic, avoided multiple attempts at seduction by sheer — and somewhat uncharacteristic — force of will, and uncovered an anti-burglary. If my time at Ladythorne had been anymore rich and full, I'd have needed serious therapy. As it was, I was simply very, very tired. I could have kissed

Jamie when he proposed that we turn in for the night.

Wendy, too, welcomed the suggestion, commenting that if she didn't get some sleep soon, she'd be too cross-eyed with fatigue to recognize the box when she saw it. While I returned the duvet to Jamie's bed, she took up the miner's lamp and headed across the hall to her room.

When she'd gone, I turned to Jamie, who was busily stashing the floor plans in a drawer in the roll-top desk, and gave him a long, hard stare. He must have felt my gaze searing the back of his neck because he left the plans half stashed and faced me.

"You weren't asleep when I knocked on your door," I said evenly. "You were studying the floor plans. But you had to make it look as though you'd been asleep, so you kept me waiting in the corridor while you rumpled the bedclothes and stripped down to your skivvies. That's why your clothes were in a heap on the floor. Right?"

He ducked his head. "I'm sorry."

"Don't apologize." I smiled ruefully. "I've guessed wrong about everything so far. It's gratifying to know that at long last I've gotten one thing right." I started for the door. "Sleep well, Jamie."

"Wait." Jamie caught up with me in two steps and put his hand on my arm. "I have a personal favor to ask of you. I realize that I have no right —"

"Just ask," I interrupted.

"Try not to judge Wendy too harshly," he said. "She was exceedingly fond of her father, and it's been difficult for her to . . . to . . ." His words trailed off, his hand slid from my arm, and he seemed to move away from me into a world of his own. "If you've known your father only as a good and honorable man, it's . . . difficult . . . to learn that he was a flawed human being. But you can't stop loving him. No matter what he did, you can't help loving him." He gazed into the middle distance for a moment. Then he blinked and was back with me again. He smiled. "Wendy's an intelligent woman. She'll figure it out. In the meantime, try not to be too hard on her."

"Since I'm an extremely flawed human being, I can't make any promises on that score," I replied. "But I'll do my best. Good night, Jamie."

"Good night."

I took my oil lamp from the mantel shelf and made my way back to my room. The fire had burned low, so I piled on more coal before changing into the white linen nightgown. I blew out the oil lamp, moved Reginald to the bedside table, and took the blue journal to bed with me, leaning back against the piled pillows, with the blankets pulled to my chin and the journal resting on my knees. The familiar lines of royal-blue ink began to move across the page as soon as I opened the journal. The fire was burning brightly enough to illuminate every word.

I'm so glad you've come to bed, Lori. I was afraid you might stay up all night, searching, and that would never do. Have you by any chance found the Peacock parure, my dear?

I closed my eyes and pictured the brown-paper-wrapped parcel tucked under the blankets atop Jamie's wardrobe.

"Yes, Dimity," I murmured. "I found the parure. . . ."

It had been a mistake to close my eyes. I didn't open them again until morning.

A series of resounding blows rattled my door five hours later.

"Madam?" Catchpole bellowed. "Got your breakfast here. You decent?"

I groaned miserably and pried my eyes open. I was lying in exactly the same position I'd been in when I'd fallen asleep, and since the blankets were still pulled to my chin, I was as decent as I'd ever been. I closed the journal and put it on the bedside table before croaking feebly, "Come in."

If there's anything a sleep-deprived person detests, it's heartiness. Catchpole was clearly one of those hideous morning people who not only rise with the sun and plow the south forty before noon, but who look down upon anyone who doesn't. I hated him passionately at that moment and deeply regretted asking him to leave his cottage.

"Good morning, madam," he roared, opening the door with one hand while balancing a four-legged bed tray on the other. "Thought I'd take you up on your invitation. Sorry to hear you're feeling poorly. Mr. Macrae tells me you plan to spend the day in bed."

"Mmmph," I replied, with a surly squint at his horrible, wide-awake visage.

If Catchpole had known how badly I wanted to eviscerate him, he would have tossed the tray to me from the doorway and fled. But since he was an egocentric, insensitive morning person, he was impervious to the tidal waves of hostility rolling toward him from the bed.

"I must say you *do* look out of sorts," he

understated, clomping loudly across the room to stand over me. "Took a chill in the night, Mr. Macrae tells me, you and Miss Walker both. Ladies shouldn't overexert themselves, is what I say. Here you go, now, madam." He placed the bed tray on my lap. "This'll put the roses back in your cheeks."

I tore my malevolent gaze from his face and focused blearily on the teak tray. It held an antique silver tea service, a delicate china cup and saucer, a pot of chutney, silverware, a linen napkin, and a large dish covered with a silver dome. I peered more closely at the tea service's silver creamer.

"Is that . . . real milk?" I asked.

"It is," Catchpole confirmed. He plucked the silver dome from the plate. "And real eggs."

Joy blossomed within me. An oozing, herb-filled omelet stretched from one edge of the plate to the other. It was garnished with fresh sprigs of rosemary and sprinkled with tarragon, and as its heady fragrance wafted into the air, my mouth, which had hitherto refused to acknowledge wakefulness, began to water uncontrollably.

"I keep a cow and some chickens in the old stables," Catchpole explained, bustling over to sweep the hearth and build a fresh fire. "The herbs are from my cottage. Thought you might enjoy a bite of something that didn't come from a packet."

"It's . . . it's beautiful," I managed, my voice trembling with emotion.

"Wish I had some orange juice to give you," he went on, "but the eggs'll do you a world of good." He finished laying the fire, then strode over to the windows. "My mother swore by the power of eggs. They're filled with vitamins and such, you know. They'll set you up a treat."

I would have retracted my murderous thoughts if Catchpole hadn't chosen that moment to fling open the drapes. To eyes grown accustomed to candlelight, the shock was extreme. My agonized screams must have caught Catchpole's attention, because he quickly closed the drapes and hastened back to the bed.

"Light bothers you, does it?" he asked, bending over me solicitously.

"Uh-huh," I mewled piteously, my palms still pressed to my eyes.

Judging by the brief glimpse I'd had of the outside world before the piercing shards of sunlight had shredded my eyeballs, it was a beautiful morning. The storm clouds had moved on, the sky was radiantly blue, and the sun's brilliance was magnified a thousandfold by the heavy mantle of snow that cloaked the valley.

"Best keep the drapes closed, then," Catchpole concluded. He picked up my oil lamp and peered intently at the reservoir. "Best refill your lamp, too. I'll take care of it, madam, if you don't mind waiting a bit. I've got to get to work with the snowplow. Should take me the best part of the day to clear the worst of the drifts, but don't you worry. Mr. Macrae said he'd look in on you and Miss Walker from time to time."

"Thank you," I whispered weakly.

"It's my pleasure." He leaned closer and dropped his voice so suddenly that I felt as if my eardrums had popped. "Have you found out who was in the attics, madam?"

"It was Wendy," I replied. "She got bored and went exploring. It's nothing to worry about."

"If you say so, madam." Catchpole straightened. "You rest up, now. I'll be off. Lots to do."

The retreating thuds of Catchpole's work boots told me that he was leaving, but it wasn't until I heard the door close that I allowed myself to peek out from behind my hands. Once reassured that the heavy drapes had effectively blocked every jagged razor of sunshine, I addressed the omelet. It tasted even better than it looked.

I was on my third cup of tea and in a much mellower mood when Jamie arrived, carrying my refilled oil lamp. He was wearing the same jeans he'd worn since he'd arrived, but he'd swapped his blue sweater for a heavy oatmeal-colored wool turtleneck. The turtleneck suited him admirably, but he seemed a bit frayed around the edges, as if he, too, found early rising a trial.

Not a morning person, I thought with some satisfaction, and thanked him for delivering the lamp. He placed it on the bedside table, then reached out to touch a fingertip to Reginald's snout.

"Who's this?" he asked.

I scanned his face for signs of ridicule, but saw only honest curiosity.

"Reginald," I replied, and threw caution to the wind. "He loves the great outdoors, so I take him along with me when I go hiking."

Jamie didn't disappoint me. "Ah, the buddy system," he said wisely. "My old Boy Scout leader would approve." He'd hardly finished the sentence when he was assaulted by a yawn that drew most of the oxygen from the room.

"Did you get any sleep at all?" I asked.

"A couple of hours," he replied. "I figured Catchpole would be up at dawn and I had to be there to feed him our story."

"You're my hero," I said, and offered him my cup of tea.

He gulped it down and handed the empty cup back to me. "Wendy's already up and dressed. She's raring to go."

"A lark, not a nighthawk," I said, with a different sort of satisfaction. "I might have known."

"Larks have their uses," Jamie pointed out.

"I can take a hint." I raised a limp wrist to my forehead. "If you'll kindly remove the tray, sir, I shall attempt to rise from my sickbed."

Jamie rolled his eyes, lifted the tray, and carried it toward the door.

"Wait a minute," I called, swinging my legs over the side of the bed. "Catchpole claims to have a snowplow. Does he?"

"It depends on what you mean by *snowplow,*" Jamie answered. "His isn't much bigger than a snow shovel — thank heavens. It'll take him eons to make a dent in the drifts. I'll keep an ear out for him, but I think he'll be too busy to bother us today."

"Good," I said. "And don't worry, Jamie.

I know we'll find the box. I can feel it in my bones."

Jamie grinned the sickly grin of a night-hawk pushed from its nest at dawn and departed, bed tray in hand.

After a brief visit to the bathroom, I dressed in my own jeans and the warm cashmere sweater I'd worn the day before. I saw no sign of Wendy while I was flitting between bathroom and bedroom, and assumed that she'd already gone up to the bell tower. I was eager to get started on the bedrooms, but there were two pieces of business I had to attend to before moving on.

First, I reached for the blue journal. A sentence appeared on the blank page before I'd so much as opened my mouth.

You were saying?

I ducked my head sheepishly. "Sorry about the delayed response, Dimity. Fatigue poleaxed me."

I suspected as much, my dear, and while it's entirely understandable, I would very much like to hear about the parure.

"I know you would," I said, "but I can't tell you everything right now. Would you settle for a condensed version?"

Any version would be preferable to none.

"Here goes," I said. "Remember the two

backpackers who landed at Ladythorne with me? They didn't come here because of the blizzard. Their fathers stole the parure and Jamie and Wendy are trying to put it back and I promised to help them and we have to work fast because once the big plows dig us out we won't have an excuse to stay and that's all I can tell you right now because I have to get moving." I took a breath. "Also, I haven't called Bill yet."

When have I ever discouraged you from ringing your husband? Telephone him at once. I can wait for a more detailed account. The parure was actually stolen, you say? And you and your companions are attempting to return it? How intriguing. Old sins cast long shadows, my dear. There's no escaping them, and the shadows shrouding Ladythorne are very old indeed. . . .

I had little doubt that Dimity would piece together the whole story before I got back to her, so I left her to her deductions and took up the cell phone. I'd gone for almost twenty-four hours without hearing the voices I loved best in the world. If that didn't constitute an emergency, nothing did.

Bill was glad to hear my voice, too, and he was filled with information on the

DeClerkes. I'd forgotten that I'd asked him to learn what he could about the family, but he hadn't. Although confined to our cottage, he'd kept his promise by employing the simple expedient of telephoning Miss Kingsley.

Miss Kingsley, a longtime friend, was the concierge at the venerable Flamborough Hotel in London and a veritable font of information on England's older and wealthier families. Her font, on this occasion, turned out to be much shallower than mine. Nothing she'd told Bill about the DeClerkes was news to me.

When he'd finished relaying Miss Kingsley's information, Bill went on to impart the unwelcome news that the country was beginning to recover from the unprecedented storm. Heathrow was creaking to life again, and fleets of heavy-duty snowplows were moving along the major arterial roads. Finch's narrow lanes remained low on the plowing priority list, but their time would come sooner than I'd hoped.

"There've been some interesting developments here at Ladythorne since we last spoke," I told him. "Nothing dangerous, just interesting. Do you think you could refrain from rescuing me for another day or so?"

Bill laughed. "Since it'll take me a full day to dig out the drifts blocking the drive, I think a delayed rescue can be arranged. Why? What's up?"

"I'm doing a good deed."

"Can I help?"

I thought for a moment, then asked, "If you were a young woman whose fiancé had just died, where would you hide the jewels you were meant to inherit on your wedding day?"

"Hmmm . . ." There was a pause as Bill applied his considerable intellect to a conundrum he could not have anticipated. "Nope, sorry, love," he said eventually, "I haven't the faintest idea, but I can't wait to hear the story behind the question."

"It's a good story," I acknowledged, "but I'm afraid you'll have to wait. I'll explain why, I promise, but not right now. Put the boys on, will you?"

I held a breathless, three-way conversation with Will and Rob, who were bursting to tell me of their plan to dig a tunnel from the cottage to Emma Harris's stables in order to make absolutely sure that the horses were safe and sound. Their utter lack of concern about my own well-being was slightly daunting, but since it argued a high degree of confidence in Mummy's survival skills, I decided to take it as a compliment.

When our conversation ended, I switched off the cell phone and cocked an ear toward the windows, distracted by an annoying noise rising from the courtyard. It was the faint roar of a motor, the first mechanized sound I'd heard since arriving at Ladythorne Abbey. I sat motionless for a moment, realizing with a faint sense of surprise how much I'd miss the abbey's stillness, then went to the windows, parted the drapes, and looked down, squinting against the dazzling glare of sunlight on snow.

There was Catchpole, in his patched canvas jacket and collection of woolly scarves, driving a plow the size of a riding mower across the courtyard, on his way to the front of the house. The path he'd cleared from his cottage to the courtyard ran like a slender thread through the vast white counterpane blanketing the landscape.

"He'll be at it till midnight," I murmured happily, and turned to take stock of my room.

The old floor plans had identified eight rooms on the second floor as family bedrooms: four for the sons who'd died in two different world wars, and one two-room suite each for Grundy and Rose. I knew that Tessa Gibbs had converted at least three of the boys' bedrooms to guest rooms because Wendy, Jamie, and I were staying in them, and I assumed she'd done the same with the rest. Since Wendy and Jamie had already searched their own rooms, I decided to start with mine, skip theirs, then go on to the two-room suites at the end of the corridor and work my way back toward the main staircase.

I spent the next two hours in my bedroom, industriously tapping the walls and rolling back the rugs to thump the floorboards. I emptied the wardrobe of clothes and ran my fingernails along every join in the wood; pulled the drawers out of the dressing table and the writing table; prodded the chairs' plump cushions; and crawled under the bed, looking for loose floorboards. I climbed up on the tables and ran my hands along the cornice boards, checked the windowsills for hollow spaces, and pressed my fingertips to every square inch of the white marble mantelpiece, hoping to activate a spring-loaded door to a secret compartment.

I found nothing.

"I've given it my best shot, Reg," I said,

after I'd restored the room to its original state. "If there's a hidey-hole in here, it's too well-hidden for me to find. Next stop: the two-room suites."

My first thought upon entering the suite on Jamie's side of the corridor was that it had been decorated to suit Grundy DeClerke's tastes. The ponderous mahogany furnishings, the many-layered drapes, and the bloodred damask wall coverings were exactly what I would have expected to find in the private sanctuary of a self-made and prosperous Victorian gentleman.

I went straight through the bedroom to the adjacent dressing room and flung open the wardrobe, hoping to discover a turn-of-the-century treasure trove of floor-length paisley dressing gowns, gold-buttoned waistcoats, and velvet-lapeled smoking jackets. I was keenly disappointed to find it filled instead with well-made but unimaginative modern clothes. A thorough search revealed that it contained nothing else.

The bedroom, by contrast, presented a wealth of possibilities. Whoever had furnished the room had evidently been obsessed with boxes because they were everywhere — on the mantel shelf, the desk, the bed tables, the occasional tables, the windowsills. Every horizontal surface seemed to exist solely to display the wildly diverse collection. I opened marquetry boxes, lacquered boxes, boxes inlaid with mother-of-pearl, teak boxes, boxes covered in gold leaf, bamboo boxes, porcelain boxes, and one large velvet-covered box that filled my heart with hope until I remembered that the parure's box was made of marble.

Mildly dispirited, I turned my attention to the floorboards, the walls, and the ponderous furniture. By the time I finished tapping, rapping, and probing my way through the vast bedroom and the spacious dressing room, my knuckles were becoming quite tender and I was fairly sure that I'd inhaled every speck of dust the weekly chars had missed. But I was completely sure I hadn't found the parure's custom-made box or a place where it might have been hidden.

I was sitting on my heels beside a hidey-holeless secretaire, sucking my bruised knuckles and feeling a bit sorry for myself, when Wendy nearly stopped my heart by flinging the door wide.

"Quick!" she cried. "Get back in bed! Catchpole's coming!"

Nineteen

Wendy fled to her room and I scampered back to mine, acutely aware of the sound of voices rising from the staircase. Jamie seemed to be doing his level best to stall Catchpole, but the old man was beginning to sound impatient. I pulled the linen nightgown over my clothes, leapt into bed, and yanked the blankets to my chin. I was still catching my breath when a familiar banging sounded on my door.

"Lunch, madam," Catchpole roared. "You awake?"

"I am now," I muttered. I glanced at my watch, realized to my amazement that it was noon, and called for Catchpole to enter.

"Beef broth and poached eggs," he announced as he placed the bed tray on my lap. "There's a little pot of caviar, too, in case you'd like to dress your eggs."

"Yum," I said, willing myself to breathe evenly.

"Mr. Macrae didn't think you'd be

hungry," Catchpole continued, "but I told him that, hungry or no, you had to eat. Got to build up your strength, I told him." He peered at me worriedly. "You're looking a bit flushed, madam. I think you may have a fever. Nasty things, fevers. Never know where they'll lead. Why don't we use that mobile of yours to ring for a doctor? They've got helicopters these days and I'm sure —"

"I don't need a doctor," I blurted, then let my head fall back against the pillows and smiled angelically. "All I need is bed rest and your good broth."

Catchpole nodded his approval. "My mother swore by the power of beef broth. You drink it down, madam. It'll chase off that fever in a trice."

"How's the plowing coming along?" I inquired.

"Slow but sure," he answered. "I've cleared the cloisters. As soon as I've had a bite to eat, I'll make a start on the courtyard."

"When you've finished, I want you to have an early supper, go straight back to your cottage, and put your feet up," I said. "There's no need to bother about bringing supper to us. Jamie will take care of it."

"Are you sure about that, madam?" said

Catchpole. "Because it's no trouble —"

"I insist," I said. "Jamie's been fooling around all day, while you've been slaving away. A stint of kitchen duty won't do him any harm."

"Might even do him some good," he conceded. "I'll see you first thing in the morning, then, madam. I hope you're feeling better by then."

"Give my best to the budgies," I said.

"I will." Catchpole paused to add coal to the fire before leaving me to my poached eggs and powerful broth.

After listening for a few minutes, I set the tray to one side, hopped out of bed, and tore off the nightgown. I had every intention of returning to the hunt, but the broth's rich aroma lured me back to the tray to make quick work of the savory meal. I'd removed the tray and was arranging the pillows on the bed to look like my reclining figure when there was a tap at my door.

I froze, pillow in hand, panic-stricken, until my brain registered the difference between the soft tap I'd just heard and Catchpole's hearty thumps.

"Jamie?" I called.

"No," Wendy replied. "It's me. Again. I'm beginning to get used to talking to you through a door. You haven't barricaded this one, have you?"

"No," I called. "Come in."

She entered the room, dressed in her slipper socks, loose black leggings, head lamp, and another lovely hand-knit sweater — this one in shades of lavender and cornflower blue flecked with gray.

"Hi," I said brightly, remembering my half-promise to Jamie. "Thanks for sounding the alarm. I'd completely lost track of time. Any luck in the bell tower?"

"Not yet," she said. "Jamie's struck out so far, too. What about you?"

"If I'd found the box, you'd know it," I told her. "I'd be dancing up the corridor whispering exultant hoorahs." I pulled the blankets over the pillows, made a few artful tucks, and stood back to survey my masterpiece of deception. "What do you think? Will it fool Catchpole?"

"It's not bad," Wendy allowed. "I'll do the same thing in my room, in case we're caught short again."

I was secretly delighted to learn that I'd thought of the trick before she had, but hid my childish glee by looking toward the sound of Catchpole's diminutive plow. The roar rising from the courtyard was a reassuring sign that he was fully occupied.

I turned back to Wendy.

"If you've spoken with Jamie, maybe you can answer a question I've been asking myself over the poached eggs," I said. "Catchpole's convinced that you and I are bedridden invalids, but what does he think Jamie's doing downstairs?"

"Playing billiards," Wendy answered. "Catchpole thinks it's the sort of thing a man can do all day, and who are we to disabuse him?"

I laughed. "I'm pretty sure I convinced Catchpole to let Jamie take care of dinner, so I don't think we'll be ambushed again. Still," I added, patting the pillows, "we can't be too careful."

Wendy wandered over to the bedside table and gazed abstractedly at Reginald. "Have you finished searching the bedrooms?"

I shook my head. "I've gone through mine and the suite on Jamie's side of the corridor."

"Would you mind coming with me for a minute?" Wendy nodded toward the door. "There's something I'd like to show you."

I gave the blankets a last tug and followed Wendy into the hall. I expected her to lead me to the bell tower, but she turned in the opposite direction and strode toward the far end of the corridor. She had a strange, unreadable expression on her face.

"I found it when I was looking for you," she explained. "It's . . . weird. I'd like to hear what you think of it." She stopped outside the two-room suite opposite Grundy's, opened the door, and stood aside to allow me to enter first.

I noticed the smell before anything else — the musty, stale odor of a room seldom aired and never dusted. Then I noticed the dead bird. It was big and black and propped against the pillows of a large four-poster bed. The bed's graceful fluted posts were draped with lengths of muslin that had once been white but were now ragged and yellowing with age. The bed's quilted white satin coverlet had taken on an unwashed, grayish hue, and loose threads dangled from its frayed hems.

Dingy oak floorboards peeked through holes in a stained and threadbare Aubusson carpet. The tattered, rose-patterned wallpaper had been inexpertly patched with strips of a different pattern, and fringed swags parted the rose-colored velvet drapes to reveal windows so filthy that they transformed bright daylight into twilight.

There was a porcelain chamber pot beneath the nightstand, a basin and ewer on the dressing table, and a blackened teakettle hanging from a pivoting fire-arm in the fireplace, mute witnesses to an impoverished self-sufficiency. The writing table held an oil lamp with a frosted globe enclosing the wick, a stamp box, an old-fashioned tortoise-shell fountain pen, a bottle of dried ink, and a half-ream of Ladythorne's ivory stationary.

Above the fireplace hung a gilt-framed oil portrait of a fine-featured young man in uniform. The only ornament on the mantel shelf was a sepia-toned wedding portrait of a couple dressed in the style of the early 1920s. The bride wore the Peacock parure.

"It's hers," I whispered. "It's Lucasta's room."

"That's what I thought." Wendy pointed at the sepia photograph. "It was probably her mother's room. My guess is that Lucasta moved in when her father died in the Blitz. I don't think anyone else has used the room since Lucasta passed away."

"Good guess." I shuddered and shrank back toward the doorway. "They could have buried the dead bird."

"It's not real," Wendy told me. "But it's

not a toy, either. Come and see."

The distant roar of Catchpole's plow invaded the twilit room as we crossed to stand beside the bed. When Wendy lifted the bird for a closer inspection, I saw at once that it wasn't a cute, cuddly stuffed animal but an exquisitely wrought piece of needlework.

The beak and legs were made of fine-grained black leather. A pair of flawless black pearls served as the eyes. The black wings, head, and body were covered with miraculously intricate beadwork sewn in a pattern that mimicked feathers. The stitches were so tiny that the seams were invisible, and the haughty cock of the bird's head gave it a personality that was the exact opposite of cuddly.

"I think it's a raven," said Wendy, returning the bird to the pillows.

"It might as well be a buzzard." I surveyed the room with a mixture of pity and distaste. "So this is where she lived out her final days — if you can call it living. The Catchpoles must have been faithful, to haul her meals up here from the kitchen."

"Catchpole said she wasn't eating much, toward the end," Wendy reminded me.

"Tea and toast and hatred," I murmured, looking at the blackened teakettle.

"Not a balanced diet."

Wendy approached the mantelpiece. She touched the framed photograph, then tilted her head back to look up at the oil portrait. "Her parents and her fiancé, I'd say. Reminders of what she'd lost."

"Fuel to keep her rage burning," I muttered. More loudly, I said, "If you ask me, she was halfway round the bend before your father ever set foot in Ladythorne."

Wendy swung around to face me. "I thought you were Lucasta's great defender."

"I am. My heart aches for her, but now that I've seen this . . ." I swept a hand through the air to encompass the room and every shabby thing in it. "I mean, millions of people had to deal with death and crushed dreams after the war, and the vast majority of them didn't shut themselves up in self-imposed squalor and write nasty letters to whoever it was they blamed for their grief." I walked to the writing desk and took up the fountain pen. "Why didn't she write nasty letters to the German air crews who strafed Dunkirk and bombed London? They robbed her of something far more precious than the Peacock parure."

"The parure was the one thing she could

hope to get back," Wendy pointed out. "Her father and her fiancé were lost to her forever."

"Even so . . ." I rolled the fountain pen between my fingers, then looked at the oil portrait. "If the theft drove Lucasta crazy, it was because she didn't have far to go in the first place."

"Thanks for trying, Lori," Wendy said, folding her arms, "but you'll never convince me that my father was blameless."

"Not blameless," I agreed. "He stole. He lied. He hurt Lucasta. But he wasn't . . . evil. He put his life on the line, and nearly lost it, fighting evil." I shrugged. "Who knows? Maybe something he did on Omaha Beach saved my dad's life. And when your father came back from the war, he worked hard, he paid the mortgage, and he raised a depressingly impressive daughter."

Wendy gave a short, mirthless laugh and ducked her head.

"I'm serious," I retorted. "Look at you. You're smart, confident, capable, strong. You're tenacious and you have courage. Maybe your father had nothing to do with how you turned out, but if he did, I'd say he was a pretty remarkable man."

Wendy stood motionless, her head

bowed. Her silence told me that her father had had a great deal to do with how she'd turned out.

Finally, she spoke. "My father was a hypocrite. He always insisted that I be honest with him, but he was never honest with me."

"Maybe he wanted you to be better than he was," I said. "And if he didn't tell you the whole truth and nothing but the truth about himself, maybe it was because he didn't want to disappoint you." I recalled the way my sons looked at me, as if I had all the answers to all the questions in the world, and trembled inwardly. "All parents keep secrets, Wendy. I suppose, deep down, we want them to. Everyone talks about the burden of expectations parents place on their children, but nobody seems to notice that it works the other way 'round as well. We don't want to know that our parents have ever been scared or helpless or bad. It's too . . . unsettling. We don't make it easy for them to tell the truth."

"And your father?" Wendy asked, her voice edged with resentment. "What were his secrets?"

"I don't know." I put the pen down on the writing table. "I never had the chance to find out."

Wendy's brow furrowed in puzzlement.

I held her gaze. "My dad died when I was three months old. I never had a chance to get really mad at him. Or to forgive him." I breathed a soft sigh. "Yet another reason to envy you."

Wendy's mouth tightened and she looked away. I thought for a moment that I'd gone too far, that she'd either tell me to mind my own blasted business or leave the room and never speak to me again. Instead, she hunched her shoulders and said gruffly, "Why hasn't Tessa Gibbs redecorated in here? It's ghoulish to leave it as it is."

I was grateful for the change of subject, relieved that I'd gotten off so lightly.

"Maybe she hasn't had time to work on it," I said. "Or maybe it's a conversation piece, a way of showing how far downhill the abbey had gone before she restored it. It's unquestionably part of Ladythorne's history." I traced a circle in the writing table's dust and thought, *The madwoman in the attic. Poor Lucasta. What a legacy.*

"Do you want to search it together?" Wendy asked, still avoiding my gaze.

"Sure." I concentrated on brushing the dust from my finger, hoping Wendy wouldn't notice how stunned I was by her offer. Camaraderie was the last thing I'd expected in return for my intrusion into an emotional arena that was clearly off limits. "I'll take the dressing room."

"I'll start in here." Wendy strode to the dresser, adding, "I'll keep an ear out for Catchpole's plow. If the engine stops, we make a run for it."

"Agreed," I said, and headed for the connecting door.

I entered the dressing room with no little trepidation, half afraid of finding a Miss Havisham–style tableau, complete with cobwebbed wedding gown and desiccated bouquet. Much to my surprise, the room was sparely furnished, neat as a pin, and reeking of mothballs. The twin sets and tweed skirts in the wardrobe were old but not ragged, and the sensible shoes lining the bottom shelf, though worn at the heels, had been meticulously and repeatedly re-soled. Good clothes, I'd been told, were made to last, and these had lasted.

The only garments that showed signs of fatigue were two flannel nightgowns and a bulky, fisherman-knit cardigan that had no doubt come in handy when the coal supplies had dwindled. I fingered the cardigan's frayed cuffs and felt a stab of pity for the sparkling girl who'd dressed so prettily for her wounded officers.

An ivory-backed brush and hand mirror lay on the dressing table beside a small porcelain box filled with hairpins. The tangle of gray hairs in the brush conjured the image of an old woman, her hair pinned in a bun, warming her hands on a teacup while contemplating what family treasure to sell next in order to cover the rising costs of overseas postage.

In the dressing table's left-hand drawer, I found a delicately embroidered handkerchief sachet. As I unfolded the smooth satin envelope, I felt the hard edges of something hidden among the lace-edged squares of silk. I slid my hand into the sachet and drew from it a book. It was bound in maroon morocco, and the pages were edged in gold. There was no title on the cover or the spine.

Scarcely daring to breathe, I turned to the first page. There, written in a neat round hand, were the words LUCASTA DECLERKE, HER DIARY. The first entry was dated January 1, 1945.

"Dear Lord," I whispered, and sank onto the chair at the dressing table. "Wendy!" I shouted. "Wendy, come in here!"

Wendy entered the dressing room at a run.

"When did your father arrive at Ladythorne?" I demanded.

"Late February, nineteen forty-five," she replied. "Why? What have you found?"

"Lucasta's diary," I told her, "for nineteen forty-five."

"Oh." Wendy scuffed a slipper sock on the floor and regarded me pensively. "I don't think we should read it, do you?"

"Not every word." I flipped through the pages until I came to the last few days of February. "Just the parts where she mentions the theft. She must have written about it in her diary. Maybe she'll tell us where to put the parure."

Wendy hung back and watched while I skimmed the pages. The entries varied in length, some containing only a few lines, some stretching to several paragraphs, but the neat round script never varied until I reached the entry dated April 25 — when the handwriting twisted and grew spikes.

"I've found it," I said, and read the passage aloud: " 'Mother visited me last night and told me that her jewels had been stolen. I checked today and it's true. I don't know how they managed it with the sentries watching, but the parure is gone. They must have waited for the dark of the moon, the devils. I will never forgive them.

NEVER!' " Shaken, I closed the diary and looked at Wendy. "That's it," I said. "That's where the entries end."

"But . . . but Lucasta's mother died before the war began," Wendy protested. "She couldn't have . . ."

"I know."

The ensuing silence seemed to last forever.

"You were right." Wendy's murmur seemed to ring out in the stillness. "Her mind was gone long before the parure was stolen. Her mother's visit must have been an hallucination."

"A pretty accurate one, though," I commented, "if it tipped Lucasta off about the theft."

"Something else must have tipped her off," Wendy stated firmly. "Something *real*. Her mother's so-called message was nothing more than a figment of her deranged imagination. The dead can't speak."

I toyed with the idea of introducing Wendy to Aunt Dimity, but quickly pushed the thought aside. Wendy's faith in her father had already been fractured. I didn't think she could cope with an expanded definition of what was real.

"What do you suppose she meant when

she wrote about the sentries and the dark of the moon?" I wondered aloud.

"Nothing," Wendy said bluntly. "More hallucinations. She was nuts, Lori. We can't trust anything she wrote in her diary. Let's get back to the job at hand." Wendy shook her head and returned to the bedroom.

"Right," I said after she'd gone, but I remained seated at the dressing table, staring at the diary. I couldn't help feeling that Lucasta was speaking to us from beyond the grave, in a language too obscure for us to decipher. Fortunately, I knew the whereabouts of a highly qualified translator.

I stood, slid the diary under my sweater, and made a beeline for the corridor, calling over my shoulder, "Bathroom break. Back in a minute."

Twenty

"And then Lucasta's diary turned up, tucked away in a handkerchief sachet," I concluded. "Listen to the final entry."

Aunt Dimity's journal lay open on the tea table in my bedroom. I stood over it while I read the final passage from the diary to her, then set the diary aside, took up the journal, and plopped onto the plump armchair.

"What do you think?" I asked.

Well. Dimity paused briefly, then carried on. *To be perfectly honest, I'm not sure what to think. You're almost certainly correct in assuming that Lucasta buried herself alive in that dreadful suite, and I can assure you that ravens formed a conspicuous part of her fiancé's coat-of-arms, but whether she made the beaded raven in his honor or he presented it to her as a love token, I can't say.*

"Dimity," I said patiently, "I'm not overly interested in Lucasta's beaded raven at the moment. I want to know what you think about her diary."

In those days it was common for a young girl to hide her diary in her handkerchief sachet.

"Fascinating," I said, with a touch of exasperation. "But I want to know what you think about the diary's contents. Was Lucasta making it up? Or did her dead mother communicate with her . . . long distance?"

I have no idea. I'm not an expert on the subject of "long-distance" communication, to use your term. I can only tell you that, while my own experience is not unique, it's not an everyday occurrence, either. Lucasta's mother may have lingered in the abbey for a time, to keep watch over her daughter, or Lucasta may have been delusional. Sadly, the preponderance of the evidence points to the latter.

"Lots of people would call me crazy if they caught me talking to a book," I countered.

But you're not crazy, my dear, or at least you're no crazier than the average human being. Lucasta, I'm afraid, was quite insane.

"Which means that we can't trust her words." I sighed dejectedly. "I was hoping the bit about sentries and the dark of the moon might lead somewhere, but I guess it's another dead end." I stood. "I'd better get back to that dreadful suite before

Wendy pries open the bathroom door."

One moment, my dear, if you please. About this search of yours . . . I've given it a good deal of consideration, and I've come to the conclusion that you're going about it the wrong way.

"What do you mean?" I asked, resuming my seat.

First of all, might I suggest that if you insist on tapping walls, you do so with the handle of a hairbrush or some other insensate object? If you continue battering your poor knuckles, you won't be able to feed yourself by the end of the day.

"Check," I said, smiling. "Hairbrush, not knuckles. Anything else?"

It strikes me that you and your friends may be looking for the wrong sort of box. We mustn't forget Lucasta's inexplicable behavior, Lori. She adamantly refused to tell anyone where the parure was hidden. Why? Might it not be because she kept the jewels in a place that had a deeply personal meaning for her, a place she couldn't bear to expose to public scrutiny? Her trousseau, perhaps? She wouldn't want strangers rummaging through her wedding clothes, now, would she?

"Her trousseau . . ." I nodded slowly. "The wedding clothes she never wore because of her fiancé's death. They'd be sacred to her. She'd never let a ham-fisted military policeman touch them, much less take them away as evidence."

Quite. And since Lucasta was supposed to receive the parure on her wedding day, it would be natural for her to keep the jewels and the clothes together in one place.

"Where?" I asked. "A wardrobe? A steamer trunk?"

A trunk would be more likely — one of the elegant, old-fashioned kind, with engraved initials and a compartment for toiletries. She would have brought it with her on her honeymoon.

"I didn't see anything like that in her dressing room," I said. "But I haven't finished searching it yet. I'll pass your idea on to Wendy and Jamie. We should be looking for a big trunk instead of a smallish box."

Just so, my dear.

"Thanks for the tip, Dimity." I set the journal aside and knelt to replenish the fire, then turned toward the bedside table to ask Reginald his opinion.

But Reginald wasn't there. Startled, I jumped to my feet and scanned the room until I noticed that someone had parted the drapes slightly. I strode to the window and saw to my relief that Reginald was sitting on the sill, gazing out over the half-plowed courtyard and the maze of snow-covered outbuildings encircling it.

"Jamie," I said, as comprehension dawned. "He stopped by, right, Reg? And he remembered what I told him about your love of the great outdoors. Remind me not to tell him that you spend most of your time on a shelf in the study at home. He'd accuse me of bunny abuse."

I gave Reginald's ears a fond twiddle and headed downstairs to find Jamie.

"A steamer trunk?" Jamie pushed his long hair back from his face and sat on his heels. I'd found him kneeling in a dark corner of the smoking room, probing the wall panels with a bread knife. "You may be on to something, Lori. It never crossed my mind to associate Lucasta's trousseau with the parure."

"It's a girl thing," I told him. I silently apologized to Dimity for stealing her thunder and went on to describe Lucasta's dreary suite and the diary I'd found hidden in the dressing table. When I finished, Jamie shook his head.

"It's a pity about the diary," he said. "It could have been useful, but I have to agree with Wendy. Lucasta was living in a dream world — or an ongoing nightmare, judging by your description of her room. Poor soul." His eyes dimmed with sadness as he bowed his head, but brightened again when he glanced up at me. "I can't believe that you and Wendy are working together."

"Astonishing, isn't it?" I rubbed the tip of my nose. "I'm glad you told me to go easy on her. She's really hurting."

"Disillusion's a difficult pill to swallow," Jamie said. "But it'll go down more easily when she remembers how much she loved her father." A low-pitched note of yearning ran through his brave words, as if he were trying to convince himself of something he found difficult to believe.

"How long did it take you to forgive your father?" I asked.

"Me? I'm still working on it." Jamie pushed himself to his feet and slid the bread knife into his back pocket, saying briskly, "I doubt that I'll find any steamer trunks in here, but there should be a box room in the service corridor. I'll check it out."

"I'll get back to Wendy," I said. "She must think I've drowned by now. Oh, and before I forget — I gave Catchpole the night off. I told him you'd bring dinner up to us."

"Good idea," said Jamie. "I'd rather have

him dozing in his cottage than dashing around the abbey. He should sleep like a log after spending the day in the fresh air."

"Speaking of the great outdoors . . ." I smiled shyly. "You're quite a guy, Jamie. Not everyone would be so understanding about Reginald."

"Your rabbit?" He grinned. "He's charming — almost as charming as you are — and I'm sure he's a wonderful listener. What's not to understand?"

I gave his arm a grateful squeeze, and made my way to the staircase.

After turning Lucasta's suite inside out, Wendy and I came to the firm conclusion that it contained nothing remotely resembling a wealthy young bride's wedding wardrobe. We hadn't found a single steamer trunk, nor had we spotted anything that might be interpreted as a jewel box fit for the parure. We indulged in a real bathroom break, to scrub away the grime we'd accumulated inspecting the grubby room, then Wendy returned to the bell tower and I continued to work my way methodically through the remaining bedrooms, substituting the hairbrush from my bedroom for my knuckles. Jamie rounded us up for dinner at seven o'clock. By then I was ready to chuck the parure into a flour sack and leave it on a pantry shelf.

"Do you mind if we eat in the kitchen?" Jamie asked. "My arms are so tired that I don't think I can lift a tray."

"What if Catchpole sees us?" Wendy asked.

"We'll tell him the broth worked," I barked. "Take me to the kitchen, *now.* If I spend one more minute in a bedroom, I'll begin frothing at the mouth."

I wasn't alone in feeling discouraged. Jamie had located the box room, but the trunks stored there had been either empty or filled with crumpled newspaper. Wendy had put her pry bar to good use, opening an assortment of wooden crates she'd found stacked in the bell tower, but the crates had yielded nothing more than endless sets of china, tarnished silver, and a few dozen second-rate watercolors.

"A bath, a bath, my kingdom for a bath," I chanted as we entered the kitchen, oil lamps in hand.

"A bubble bath," Wendy chimed in, "followed by a nice, relaxing massage."

"I hesitate to offer a massage," said Jamie, "but there should be enough hot water to provide baths all round."

"What's the point?" I gazed mournfully

at the streaks of dust marring my beautiful, butter-soft sweater. "We'll just get filthy again. I assume the plan is to work through the night."

"Unfortunately, yes." Jamie yawned. "But I'm sure a meal will perk us up."

I brewed a pot of tea and helped Wendy set the table while Jamie artfully transformed a bowl of Catchpole's eggs into a massive omelet supplemented by nibbly bits from the larder. After we'd polished off the omelet, Jamie won our undying adoration by making another batch of apricot compote.

"I asked Catchpole how to make it when I was stalling him on the stairs at lunchtime," he told us. "I couldn't think of anything else to say. It's as easy as pie — much easier, in fact, because it doesn't require a crust."

The compote, and the half-hour break it gave us while it baked, did much to restore our collective sense of well-being.

"Have you noticed how the house seems to expand as we search it?" I asked as we carried the dishes to the sink. "I'm willing to swear that my bedroom had stretched to at least ten thousand square feet by the time I'd finished with it."

"I had the same trouble with the bell

tower," Wendy acknowledged. "It must be as tall as the Empire State Building by now."

"Did you know that steamer trunks breed?" Jamie added conversationally. "They're like rabbits. You start with a pair and end up with a multitude."

I could tell by Wendy's fidgeting that she was anxious to get back to work, so I sent her on her way, assuring her that I considered dish washing the next best thing to having a bath. When Jamie offered to give me a hand, I ordered him in no uncertain terms to sit down, finish his tea, and relax. In my book, anyone who made dinner was exempt from washing up. Apart from that, Jamie had gotten less sleep than Wendy and I, and he'd spent a good chunk of the day dealing with Catchpole. He deserved an extra ration of rest.

He clearly needed one. By the time I finished filling the sink, he was slumped over the table, his head pillowed on his arms, dead to the world. My brain must have taken a catnap, too, because I was startled into full wakefulness when the back door swung open and Catchpole clomped into the room, shedding snow from his hobnailed boots with every step.

I shushed him furiously and pointed to

Jamie, who hadn't stirred. "Walk softly, will you? And keep your voice down."

The old man's tread was unexpectedly light as he approached the sink. "Feeling better, madam?"

"The broth worked," I replied automatically.

"Knew it would." Catchpole unwound his woolly scarves, unbuttoned his canvas jacket, and reached for a towel. "Here, let me help. Many hands make light work, my mother used to say."

It was a strange sensation, to be sharing such a homely chore with a man who had once threatened me with a shotgun, but when I remembered the injured owl and the adopted bluetits, I stopped marveling. There was more to Catchpole than met the eye. As that thought crossed my mind, it sparked another, and I glanced at Catchpole with renewed interest. It had suddenly dawned on me that, in our zeal to keep the old man in the dark, Jamie, Wendy, and I had overlooked his potential as a source of information.

I looked over my shoulder. Neither the slosh of dishwater nor the occasional rattle of plate against plate had roused Jamie from his slumber. I doubted that a quiet conversation would disturb him. I'd have to be circumspect, of course. Quizzing Catchpole directly about the jewels would only set off his inner burglar alarm, and I wasn't in the mood to squelch another diatribe about thieving Yanks.

"While I was lying in bed today," I began, "I couldn't help thinking about Miss DeClerke."

"Stands to reason," said Catchpole. "Miss DeClerke was the sort of woman who made people think."

"I'm sure she was," I agreed, and passed a dripping bowl to him. "The thing is, I was itching to get up after only a few hours. It seems incredible to me that Miss DeClerke spent years confined to one room."

A reminiscent gleam lit Catchpole's eyes. "She didn't spend all of her time in her room, madam. She'd go out at night, sometimes, and wander about the grounds."

"Is that right?" I looked thoughtfully at the cluster of outbuildings framed by the Gothic windows above the long stone sink. "Did she go anywhere in particular?"

When Catchpole was slow to answer, I gave him a sidelong glance and saw to my astonishment that a darker shade of red had risen beneath the wind-and sunburn coloring his grizzled face. For some reason, the old man was blushing.

"Not so's you'd notice, madam. No particular place." He shifted uncomfortably from one foot to another, his hobnails clicking on the tiles.

"Huh? What?" Jamie raised his head and blinked blearily in our direction. "Catchpole? What're you doing here? Thought you'd gone back to your place."

Catchpole seemed relieved by the interruption. "Popped in to make sure you'd given the ladies their dinner, Mr. Macrae."

"Jamie gave us a beautiful dinner," I said. "He even made apricot compote for us. It wasn't as tasty as yours, but it was awfully good."

"I expect you don't use a range too often, eh, Mr. Macrae?" Catchpole asked.

"First time," said Jamie.

"That'd explain it. Practice up and your compote'll soon be as good as mine." Catchpole hurriedly dried the last plate and returned it to its place on the white dresser. "I heard good news on the radio, madam. They'll be sending the big plows our way sometime tomorrow. I'm sure you'll be glad to go home."

"Absolutely," I said, forcing a smile. "Can't wait."

"I'll be off, then. Good night to you both." Catchpole draped his damp towel over the drying rack, rewound his scarves, and let himself out the back door.

I watched the old man until he disappeared into the night, then let my gaze rove over the irregular roof lines of the squat buildings on the far side of the courtyard.

"Is there an outhouse out there?" I asked.

"An outhouse? As in privy?" Jamie stretched the kinks out of his arms and shoulders, then joined me at the sink. "Why do you ask?"

"Catchpole told me that Lucasta used to wander around outside at night," I explained. "When I asked him where she went, he hemmed and hawed and went red in the face."

Jamie waggled his eyebrows suggestively. "Maybe she visited his cottage for reasons a gentleman wouldn't care to reveal."

"Not a chance," I said. "Catchpole has old-fashioned ideas about his station in life. I think maybe she went someplace he'd be too embarrassed to mention to me, like an outhouse."

Jamie stroked his beard and leaned forward to peer through the windows. "There was a schematic of the grounds among the floor plans in the map case. If I recall correctly, the drawing shows a wash house, a bake house, a brewery — every large estate had its own in those days — and the stables, where Catchpole keeps his livestock. Beyond the courtyard, there's his cottage, of course, and —"

I cut him off with a sharp intake of breath.

"Lori?" he said, eyeing me curiously. "Lori, what is it? Do you think the parure is hidden in one of the outbuildings?"

The hairs rose on the back of my neck.

"Find Wendy," I said. "Bring her to the kitchen. And tell her to put on her hiking boots."

Jamie must have sensed the urgency behind my quiet words because he didn't ask anymore questions. He simply took off at a run, promising to return as quickly as possible.

When he'd gone, I continued to stare, aghast, into the darkness. I knew beyond any possibility of doubt where the Peacock parure had been hidden. And I knew it would break Jamie's heart.

Twenty-one

I gave Jamie a head start before going upstairs. I stopped in Wendy's room, and his, to retrieve their parkas and the Peacock parure, and to study the schematic of the grounds. Then I went to my own room.

Reginald was still sitting on the windowsill, gazing out.

"You knew," I said numbly. "You were trying to tell me where to look, but I didn't catch the hint. Forgive me, old bean."

I lifted Reginald from the sill and placed him on the slipper chair, where he could warm himself before the fire, then took my hat, gloves, and lightweight down jacket from the wardrobe and returned to the kitchen.

Jamie and Wendy were already there. I was glad to see that Wendy had brought her pry bar.

"Jamie tells me we're going privy-dipping," Wendy said brightly, but the smile faded from her face when she caught sight of my somber expression.

I motioned for them to sit down, piled the parkas and the brown-paper-wrapped parcel on the table, and ran my fingers through my hair. I felt the need to prepare them for the final leg of their long and painful journey, but wasn't sure how to go about it. I couldn't bring myself to blurt out what I knew. I had to soften the blow, somehow.

"I'm no expert on fathers," I said slowly, sitting across the table from them, "but I know, by knowing you, that yours must have been pretty wonderful. I have to believe that they stole the parure because the war clouded their judgment, or they were bewitched by Ladythorne — or maybe even because they hoped one day to make life easier for you.

"If your fathers hadn't been fundamentally decent guys, the theft wouldn't have haunted them. But . . ." I searched for the right words, and found them. "But old sins cast long shadows, and their sin cast a shadow over the rest of their lives. In the end it killed Wally, and it tortured James in ways I can't begin to imagine. I know how angry you are with those two young men, but I hope you'll find a way to forgive them. Because they never forgave themselves."

Coals toppled inside the range. An oil lamp sputtered. Wendy's gaze had turned inward, but Jamie's never wavered.

"You're leading up to something," he said. "What is it? Do you know where the parure was hidden?"

I picked up the parcel and reached for my jacket.

"Put on your parkas," I said, "and follow me."

The night air was bitterly cold. The snow was crisp under our boots. The stars shone like pinpoints of ice in the raven-black sky, and a rising moon silvered the snow as we trudged, single file, along the narrow path Catchpole had carved with his plow.

"See how the moonlight turns night into day?" I said in a low-voiced murmur. "That's why they had to wait for the dark of the moon. It was part of the treasure hunt, part of the game. They had to avoid being caught by the sentries the army had posted to protect the convalescent home."

We passed the bake house, the wash house, the brewery, the stables.

"There was no need to dodge Catch-pole's cottage." I lowered my voice further still as the snow-covered pines came into view. "Mr. Catchpole had gone away to war. Mrs. Catchpole and her young son had gone north to Shropshire, to help run the family farm. Their cottage was empty."

When the plowed path ended, I guided them along a snow-covered trail that wound through the trees to a clearing. There, in the center of a wide circle of pale beeches, stood an edifice as eccentric as Ladythorne itself. It was luminous in the moonlight, made of polished white marble carved to look like a great square-topped tent, its sloping roof rising to a central peak, its walls falling in soft folds to the ground, its shadowy entrance flanked by a pair of imposing statues that made my flesh creep. The two looming, anonymous figures, shrouded in hooded capes, stood facing each other across the shadowy gap, heads bowed, as if in eternal mourning.

Jamie looked at me questioningly. "The mausoleum?"

"The marble box," I said. "Lucasta had no heirs. I think she planned to take the parure with her when she died."

Beside me, I heard Jamie gasp.

"Grave-robbers," he whispered. "Dear God, they were *grave-robbers.*"

I drew a shuddering breath and felt dread rise within me. Although I had every intention of returning the parure to its rightful owner, I wasn't sure I had the nerve to open a two-year-old grave.

The snow crunched crisply as Wendy took a step forward, her gaze fixed on the mausoleum.

"They were young and shattered," she said evenly, as though in response to Jamie's horrified whisper. "They'd seen their buddies' mutilated corpses buried in sand, in mud, or left in the rain to rot." She pointed the pry bar at the gleaming white tomb. "Here, death's wrapped in a pretty package — how could they take it seriously? It was just a stage set to them, part of the game." Her hand fell to her side. "After everything they'd been through, everything they'd seen, it must have been pure joy to feel such innocent chills. Like . . . like telling yourself spooky stories when you know Dad's up the hall, ready to protect you. Dad knew he was safe here. He could afford to play childish games. He didn't have to be afraid anymore."

She blinked rapidly, gripped the pry bar with both hands, and started toward the gap between the ghostly statues. Jamie followed and I trailed after them, trying hard to blink away my own tears before they froze on my face. It was the first time I'd heard Wendy call her father "Dad."

We hadn't needed our flashlights while walking the moonlit path, but as we passed between the shrouded figures, we switched them on. The mausoleum's door had been carved to resemble an intricately patterned rug, the kind bedouins used to cover a tent's floor. Wendy bent low to examine the lock, then stood back, grasped the handle, and pulled. Icy fingers seemed to brush my face as the door swung outward.

We moved as lightly as disembodied spirits across the threshold, through a small anteroom lined with white marble benches, and into a chamber that had clearly been built to hold more generations of DeClerkes than it ever would. The chamber's walls were smooth and vertical, but the ceiling rose to a central peak.

Grundy and Rose shared a tomb beneath the peak. Their white marble effigies, clad in medieval garb, lay side by side atop the white sepulcher, hands folded in prayer and faces turned heavenward. On the wall to the left, marble tablets memorialized three of their four sons. The tablets' gold lettering spoke poignantly of the boys' gallantry and the graves they occupied in the foreign fields of Flanders and northern France.

Lucasta's mother and father had no effigies on their tombs. Their mortal remains were enclosed in simple oblong blocks of marble, in which their names had been carved above the dates of their births and untimely deaths. Lucasta's tomb was equally unadorned, apart from a few fresh sprigs of rosemary.

"For remembrance," I said under my breath, and recalled the pots of herbs in Catchpole's cottage.

A fourth tablet had been set into the wall above Lucasta's tomb. Our beams converged on it like searchlights, illuminating the curious inscription:

P. P. DECLERKE, ESQ.
1897–1940

I took note of the telltale initials and dates and nearly wept with relief. I wouldn't have to test my nerves after all.

"Eighteen ninety-seven," I said shakily. "Queen Victoria's Golden Jubilee. The first time Rose wore the parure."

"Nineteen forty." Jamie's hushed whisper echoed eerily in the chamber. "Dunkirk — and the wedding that never took place."

Wendy laid her pry bar on the floor and

slid her fingers around the edge of the tablet.

"It's hinged," she said, and gave the tablet a firm tug.

It swung away from the wall, revealing a hollow cavity that served as the receptacle for a gold-hinged box made of luminous white marble. While Jamie slid the box from the niche, I passed the brown-paper-wrapped parcel to Wendy and backed away, reluctant to intrude on a moment that belonged to them alone.

Jamie set the box on Lucasta's tomb, raised the lid, and paused.

"There's an envelope." His puzzled words echoed off the smooth walls as he lifted the ivory envelope into the light.

Two words had been written on it. I recognized the neat, round hand even from a distance, although I'd seen it only once before.

" 'Thank you,' " Jamie read aloud.

When he slid a single folded sheet of ivory stationary from the envelope, I couldn't keep myself from moving to his side to read the message sent from beyond the grave:

Whoever you are, and wherever you've come from, thank you for bringing my treasure back to me. You and I know, now, what really happened all those many long years ago. If you didn't, you wouldn't be reading this, and I, of course, have gone to a place where everything is known.

I imagine you as a young man, a son or a grandson struggling to come to terms with a painful truth. Try to remember that it isn't the whole truth. No man should be judged by his misdeeds alone. Where there was love, let there be love still. These are lessons learned too late by a dying woman. I hope that you will be wiser than she was.

Lucasta Eleanora DeClerke

Jamie stared at the letter for a long time, reading and rereading it, as if memorizing each curving line of script. Then he folded the ivory sheet, put it back in the envelope, and offered it to Wendy, who waved it off. Perhaps she understood that he needed it more than she did.

"You keep it," she said. "I'll always know where to find it."

Jamie hesitated only a moment before tucking the envelope into his parka.

Wendy placed the parcel beside the marble box. As she unfolded the plain brown paper, the diamonds caught our flashlights' beams and tossed them into the air, show-

beams and tossed them into the air, showering the cold white marble with a thousand glittering sparks. The shimmering flecks danced and tumbled over the tombs as the individual pieces of the parure were transferred from the humble packet to their final resting place.

Wendy laid the tiara in the perfectly carved crescent in the center of the box, and Jamie placed the earrings in the two pear-shaped depressions designed to hold them. The brooches followed, then the bracelets, the choker, and, last of all, the magnificent necklace, encircling the rest of the parure in a halo of heavenly radiance. I felt a flutter of regret as Wendy closed the lid, but a few elusive gleams seemed to linger even after the jewels were out of sight.

Jamie slid the box into the niche, closed the tablet, and turned to place his hand upon the tomb, saying, "Rest in peace, Lucasta."

"Rest in peace, Dad," Wendy added, cocking an eye toward the ceiling's central peak.

"Father," Jamie murmured, bowing his head, "rest in peace."

Twenty-two

I sat in the plump armchair with the journal resting in my lap, and Reginald cradled in the crook of my arm. The others had tumbled off to bed in a haze of exhaustion, but although I'd taken a deliciously long, hot bath and changed into the linen nightgown, I couldn't let go of the day.

I replayed scenes from it over and over in my mind: the lengths of tattered muslin hanging from Lucasta's bed, the beaded raven propped against her pillows, the mausoleum's ghostly guardians, the flecks of light flitting like fairies across the polished white walls. I didn't have to close my eyes to hear again the tenderness in Wendy's voice when she uttered the word *Dad,* and the tremble in Jamie's as he laid his father's troubled soul to rest.

I tried to describe the scenes to Dimity, knowing that I couldn't do them justice but hoping that, by speaking them aloud, I'd fix each separate moment in my memory. When I reached the end of the tale, I moved the oil lamp closer to the chair and watched as Dimity's handwriting looped across the page.

It was clever of you to connect the parure with the mausoleum, Lori. May I ask what inspired such a penetrating revelation?

"Catchpole," I replied. "He told me that Lucasta used to walk outside at night, but he wouldn't tell me where she went. Then I remembered what you said about Lucasta keeping the jewels in a place that had a deeply personal meaning for her. When I put those two things together with Jamie's vague description of a marble box, the answer just sort of jumped out at me."

It's not difficult to understand why Catchpole would be reluctant to admit that his mistress entered the mausoleum on a regular basis. He would consider it further evidence of her madness, which, of course, it was. I should have known that Lucasta would hide the parure among the dead. A burial chamber is, in hindsight, the most logical place for her to choose.

I lifted an eyebrow. "Don't you think it's a little . . . creepy?"

It's a great deal more than a little creepy, my dear, but that doesn't make it any less logical. The bullets that killed Lucasta's young man killed something in her as well. She be-

lieved she'd never marry, never have a daughter upon whom to bestow the jewels. To her mind, the Peacock parure, which should have marked the beginning of a new and wonderful chapter in her life, served instead only to remind her of what might have been. When she entombed the parure, she enclosed with it her ability to love, to hope, to believe in the possibility of happiness.

"In her letter, she spoke of love," I said wistfully. "And she seemed to speak of forgiveness. I'd like to think that she came to her senses before she died, that her generous spirit fought its way to the surface and overcame her anger."

It's possible. An appointment with the Grim Reaper tends to focus the mind on those things that are truly important. Perhaps she learned, in the end, that the only way to rest in peace is to live in it.

A floorboard creaked in the corridor. Startled, I laid the journal aside and got to my feet.

"Lori?" Jamie called softly. "I've brought cocoa."

I hastened to open the door. Jamie stood there, dressed in the same clothes he'd worn throughout the day, looking apologetic and carrying a tray that held three steaming mugs.

"Hullo," he said, looking past me. "I wouldn't have bothered you if I thought you were asleep, but I was sure I heard voices."

"Just one voice. Mine." As I drew him into the room, I held Reginald up for him to see. "Reg isn't exactly a chatterbox."

"A good listener, though." Jamie smiled and set the tray on the tea table. "Does he like cocoa?"

I placed Reginald on the bedside table and shook my head emphatically. "He's allergic to it. That's why he has to give all of his chocolate to me."

Jamie swayed on his feet as he laughed. I ran to his side, eased him into the plump armchair, and told him that he should be in bed. He didn't argue.

"I've tried, but I can't seem to sleep," he said. "It's absurd, I know . . ."

"Maybe not." I sat in the slipper chair, curled my legs under me, and studied his tired face. "Your life's been out of kilter for . . . how long?"

"Four years," he replied. "Ever since Father's illness became debilitating."

"Those four years ended tonight," I told him. "It'll take some getting used to."

Jamie lifted a mug of cocoa from the tray and cradled it in his hands. "I *do* feel strange," he murmured. "My life's revolved around my father for so long . . . I'm not sure what to do next."

"Read a book," I said promptly. "Eat bonbons. Climb a mountain. Come meet my sons. After a day with them, I *guarantee* that you'll be able to sleep." I reached for a mug. "What I mean is, you've got your life back again, Jamie. Whatever you do, don't waste it."

"I could do serious damage to a box of bonbons," he said thoughtfully.

"That's the spirit!" I raised my mug to toast him, then turned at the sound of yet another knock on my door.

Wendy stuck her head into the room. "Is this a private party, or can anyone join?"

"I never realized that insomnia could be contagious," I said, beckoning to her to come in. "Have some cocoa. It's still piping hot."

When Wendy took up her customary position on the floor, I grabbed an armload of pillows from the bed and tossed them to her. She curled herself among them like a cat.

"I've been worrying about the parure," she said after a warming sip of cocoa. "Do you think it's safe where it is? There's no lock on the marble box or the wall tablet, and the mausoleum's door was unlocked. What if one of Tessa Gibbs's celebrity pals gets drunk and decides to poke around in there?"

"I'll give Catchpole his shotgun tomorrow," I said, with grim determination. "And I'll tell him to load it this time."

"Or," Jamie suggested mildly, "you could ask your husband to have a chat with Tessa. He can advise her about the legal ramifications of leaving national historic sites unprotected."

"I like my solution better," I grumbled, "but yours is probably more sensible. I'll talk to Bill when I get home."

"Home," Jamie echoed. "Is that where you're going, Wendy?"

"Not until I finish my hike," she replied. "There's a little farm about ten miles from here where they raise Wensleydale sheep. Have you ever seen Wensleydales? The wool is a deep, rich, dark brown — very attractive." She looked at me over the rim of her mug. "I think the color'll suit you, Lori."

"Me?" I said, taken aback.

"I've noticed you eyeing my sweaters," she said. "Look for yours in the mail around Easter." She grinned. "Not what you expected from Miss Rude, right?"

"You? Miss Rude? Ha." I tossed my head. "I hate to break it to you, Wendy, but your attempts to insult me were feeble, at best."

"Hey," she objected. "I spent a lot of time practicing those lines."

"Pathetic," I said. "If Jamie hadn't kept cutting me off, I would have shown you what it means to be *spontaneously* mean and nasty. It comes naturally to some of us. It's one of *my* gifts."

"I couldn't agree more," said Jamie. "Only a truly mean and nasty woman would offer help in return for attempted seduction and a stream of unwarranted insults."

"Piffle," I retorted. "I was expecting to be knocked over the head and dumped in the blanket chest. Compared to that, what you guys did was downright wholesome. If you think I'm going to judge you by your misdeeds, you're very much mistaken."

Jamie caught the reference. He gazed solemnly into the fire, then set his cup aside and reached out to take hold of my hand and Wendy's.

"Where there's friendship," he said, "let there be friendship always."

"Always," I echoed, and Wendy nodded.

Jamie released us, but the bond remained, though I was forced to pummel Wendy mercilessly with a pillow when she mentioned casually that she not only played the piano, but had recently learned to play an exotic instrument called the gamelan. It irked me no end to think that the only thing she *didn't* do well was to be naturally mean and nasty.

We talked on into the night, until our yawns outnumbered even partial sentences. After Jamie and Wendy had gone off to their rooms to seek sweet oblivion, I turned down my oil lamp and fell into bed. The last conscious thought to cross my mind was that I'd found a pair of diamonds at Ladythorne I'd never return.

"Thieving Yank," I murmured, smiling, and drifted off to sleep.

Epilogue

I was the last Yank to leave Ladythorne. Wendy set off shortly after breakfast the next day, on foot, determined to enjoy the rest of her time in England. An hour later, Jamie caught a lift with a snowplow driver who would eventually drop him off in Oxford, where he planned to spend a few weeks reconnecting with old friends. I felt a pang of sorrow as I waved good-bye to each of them, but it was short-lived. I had no doubt that I would see them both again.

Catchpole was so pleased to have his shotgun back that he offered to introduce me to his cow. As he led me to the stables, I noticed a softness in the air and a handful of narcissi blooming in a stone trough in a corner of the courtyard.

"The wind's changed," Catchpole told me. "It's coming up from the south now, gentle as you please. A healing wind, my mother called it, a wind to chase away the frost and bring life back to the land."

I looked toward the south and wondered: Had the healing wind come by chance? Or had it been summoned to celebrate the resurgence of life in a place once held fast in the frosty grip of grief?

Come now, Lori. Aunt Dimity's words returned to me, curling and looping before my mind's eye as clearly as if the journal lay open before me. *You were caught in a storm that wasn't forecast, placed on a path you'd no intention of taking, and led to a house you never knew existed. Do you truly believe you came here by chance?*

I was no longer so sure of my answer.

It wasn't until after lunch that my patience was rewarded by the welcome sight of my gallant husband, riding to my rescue in our canary-yellow Range Rover. Catchpole carried my day pack to the car for me, and stood waving to us with his shotgun as Bill and I started our journey home.

"Is that the crazy caretaker?" Bill asked.

I thought of the sprigs of rosemary on Lucasta's tomb.

"He's not crazy," I replied. "At least, he's no crazier than the average human being."

We splashed through runnels of melt water as we sped up the narrow lane, and cascades of droplets fell from the trees to splash against the Rover's windshield. A fuzz of new buds softened the outlines of each overhanging branch, and an occasional green shoot could be seen emerging from the lane's steep banks.

"Looks like a spring thaw is on the way," Bill commented.

"It can't come soon enough for me," I said, but as we passed between the ivy-clad gate posts I knew in my heart that I wouldn't trade a hundred spring thaws for the days I'd spent at Ladythorne, snowbound.

Catchpole's Apricot Compote

Serves four

2 cups (½ pound) canned apricots
2 tablespoons brown sugar
juice and grated rind of ½ lemon
½ cup macaroon (or sugar cookie) crumbs

Preheat oven to 350 degrees Fahrenheit

Arrange layers of fruit in a deep baking dish, sprinkling each layer with brown sugar, lemon rind, and lemon juice. Pour the reserved juice from the can(s) on top, sprinkle with crumbs, and bake 35 minutes. Serve warm or cold, preferably with heavy cream.

NEW TECUMSETH
Property
of
PUBLIC LIBRARY